THE COLLECTORS

Being Cases mostly under the
Ninth and Tenth Commandments

FRANK JEWETT MATHER, Junr.

The Collectors

Frank Jewett Mather

PO Box 2211
Fairfield, IA 52556
www.1stworldlibrary.org
First Edition

LCCN: 2004195618

Softcover ISBN: 1-4218-0439-5
Hardcover ISBN: 1-4218-0339-9
eBook ISBN: 1-4218-0539-1

The Collectors
contributed by Tim, Ed & Rodney
in support of
1st World Library Literary Society

Comprising a *Ballade*, wherein the Wrongfulness of Art Collecting is conceded, and as well Certain Stories: *Campbell Corot*, which recounts the career of an able and candid Picture Forger. *The del Puente Giorgione*, which tells of an artful Great Lady and an Artless Expert. *The Lombard Runes*, a mere interlude, but revealing a certain duplicity in Professional Seekers for Truth. *Their Cross*, so called from an inanimate Object of Price which wrought Woe to a well meaning New York Couple. *The Missing St Michael*, a tale of Italianate Americans which is full of Vanities and, though alluring to the Sophisticated, quite unfit for the Simple Reader. *The Lustred Pots*, again a mere interlude, but of a grim sort, as it grazes the Sixth Commandment and *The Balaklava Coronal*, which, notwithstanding its exotic title, is mostly of our own People, showing the Triumph of a resourceful Dealer over two Critics and a Captain of Industry. To which seven stories are added some *Reflections upon Art Collecting*, setting forth Excuses and Palliations for a Practice usually regarded as Pernicious.

FOREWORD

Of the seven stories of art collecting that make up this book "Campbell Corot" and the "Missing St. Michael" first appeared under the pseudonym of Francis Cotton, in "Scribner's Magazine," and are now reprinted by its courteous permission. Similar acknowledgment is due the "Nation" for allowing the sketch on art collecting to be republished. Many readers will note the similarity between the story "The del Puente Giorgione" and Paul Bourget's brilliant novelette, "La Dame qui a perdu son Peintre." My story was written in the winter of 1907, and it was not until the summer of 1911 that M. Bourget's delightful tale came under my eye. Clearly the same incident has served us both as raw material, and the noteworthy differences between the two versions should sufficiently advise the reader how little either is to be taken as a literal record of facts or estimate of personalities.

CONTENTS

A BALLADE OF ART COLLECTORS

Oh Lord! We are the covetous.
  Our neighbours' goods afflict us sore.
From Frisco to the Bosphorus
  All sightly stuff, the less the more,
We want it in our hoard and store.
  Nor sacrilege doth us appal -
Egyptian vault--fane at Cawnpore -
  Collector folk are sinners all.

Our envoys plot *in partibus*.
  They've small regard for chancel door,
Or Buddhist bolts contiguous
  To lustrous jade or gold galore
Adorning idol squat or tall -
  These be strange gods that we adore -
Collector folk are sinners all.

Of Romulus Augustulus
  The signet ring I proudly wore.
Some rummaging *in ossibus*
  I most repentantly deplore.
My taste has changed; I now explore
  The sepulchres of Senegal
And seek the pots of Singapore -
  Collector folk are sinners all.

Lord! Crave my neighbour's wife! What for?
  I much prefer his crystal ball
From far Cathay. Then, Lord, ignore
  Collector folk who're sinners all.

CAMPBELL COROT

The Academy reception was approaching a perspiring and vociferous close when the Antiquary whispered an invitation to the Painter, the Patron, and the Critic. A Scotch woodcock at "Dick's" weighs heavily, even against the more solid pleasures of the mind, so terminating four conferences on as many tendencies in modern art, and abandoning four hungry souls, four hungry bodies bore down an avenue toward "Dick's" smoky realm, where they found a quiet corner apart from the crowd. It is a place where one may talk freely or even foolishly - one of those rare oases in which an artist, for example, may venture to read a lesson to an avowed patron of art. All the way down the Patron had bored us with his new Corot, which he described at tedious length. Now the Antiquary barely tolerated anything this side of the eighteenth century, the Painter was of Courbet's sturdy following, the Critic had been writing for a season that the only hope in art for the rich was to emancipate themselves from the exclusive idolatry of Barbizon. Accordingly the Patron's rhapsodies fell on impatient ears, and when he continued his importunities over the Scotch woodcock and ale, the Painter was impelled to express the sense of the meeting.

"Speaking of Corot," he began genially, "there are certain misapprehensions about him which I am fortunately able to clear up. People imagine, for instance, that he haunted the woods about Ville d'Avray. Not at all. He frequented the gin - mills in Cedar Street. We are told he wore a peasant's blouse and sabots; on the contrary, he sported a frock - coat and congress gaiters. His long clay pipe has passed into legend, whereas he actually smoked a tilted Pittsburg stogy. We speak of him by the operatic name of Camille; he was prosaically called Campbell. You think he worked out of doors at rosy dawn; he painted habitually in an air - tight attic by lamplight."

As the Painter paused for the sensation to sink in, the Antiquary murmured soothingly, "Get it off your mind quickly, Old Man," the Critic remarked that the Campbells were surely coming, and the Patron asked with nettled dignity how the Painter knew.

"Know?" he resumed, having had the necessary fillip. "Because I knew him, smelled his stogy, and drank with him in Cedar Street. It was some time in the early '70s, when a passion for Corot's opalescences (with the Critic's permission) was the latest and most knowing fad. As a realist I half mistrusted the fascination, but I felt it with the rest, and whenever any of the besotted dealers of that rude age got in an 'Early Morning' or a 'Dance of Nymphs,' I was there among the first. For another reason, my friend Rosenheim, then in his modest beginnings as a marchand - amateur, was likely to appear at such private views. With his infallible tact for future salability, he was already unloading the Institute, and laying in Barbizon. Find what he's buying now, and I'll tell you the next fad."

The Critic nodded sagaciously, knowing that Rosenheim, who now poses as collecting only for his pleasure, has already begun to affect the drastic productions of certain clever young Spanish realists.

"Rosenheim," the Painter pursued, "really loved his Corot quite apart from prospective values. I fancy the pink silkiness of the manner always appeals to Jews, recalling their most authentic taste, the eighteenth - century Frenchman. Anyhow, Rosenheim took his new love seriously, followed up the smallest examples religiously, learned to know the forgeries that were already afloat - in short, was the best informed Corotist in the city. It was appropriate, then, that my first relations with the poet - painter should have the sanction of Rosenheim's presence."

Lingering upon the reminiscence, the Painter sopped up the last bit of anchovy paste, drained his toby, and pushed it away. The rest of us settled back comfortably for a long session, as he persisted. "Rosenheim wrote me one day that he had got wind of a Corot in a Cedar Street auction room. It might be, so his news went, the pendant to the one he had recently bought at the Bolton sale. He suggested we should go down together and see. So we joggled down Broadway in the 'bus, on what looked rather like a wild - goose chase. But it paid to keep the run of Cedar Street in those days; one might find anything. The gilded black walnut was pushing the old mahogany out of good houses; Wyant and Homer Martin were occasionally raising the wind by ventures in omnibus sales; then there were old masters which one cannot mention because nobody would believe. But that particular morning the Corot had no real competitor; its radiance fairly filled the entire junk - room. Rosenheim was in raptures. As luck would have it, it was indeed the companion - piece to his, and his it should be at all costs. In Cedar Street, he reasonably felt, one might even hope to get it cheap. Then began our *duo* on the theme of atmosphere, vibrancy, etc. - brand new phrases, mind you, in those innocent days. As Rosenheim for a moment carried the burden alone, I stepped up to the canvas and saw, with a shock, that the paint was about two days old. Under what conditions I wondered - for did I not know the ways of paint - could a real Corot have come over so fresh? I more than scented trickery. A sketch over-painted - or it seemed above the quality of a sheer forgery - or was the case worse than that? Meanwhile not a shade of doubt was in Rosenheim's mind. As I canvassed the possibilities his *sotto-voce* ecstasies continued, to the vast amusement, as I perceived, of a sardonic stranger who hovered unsteadily in the background. This ill-omened person was clad in a statesmanlike black frock-coat with trousers of similar funereal shade. A white lawn tie, much soiled, and congress gaiters, much frayed, were appropriate details of a costume inevitably topped off with an army slouch hat that had long lacked the brush. He was immensely long and sallow, wore a drooping moustache vaguely blonde, between the unkempt curtains of which a thin cheroot pointed heavenward. As he walked nervously up and down, with a suspiciously stilted gait, he observed Rosenheim with evident scorn and the picture with a strange pride. He was not merely odd, but also offensive, for as Rosenheim whispered *'Comme c'est beau*!' there was an unmistakable snort; when he continued, *'Mais c'est exquis*!' the snort broadened into a mighty chuckle; while as he concluded 'Most luminous!' the chuckle became articulate, in an 'Oh, shucks!' that could not be ignored.

"'You seem to be interested, sir,' Rosenheim remarked. 'You bet!' was the terse response. 'May I inquire the cause of your concern?' Rosenheim continued placidly. With a most exasperating air of willingness to please, the stranger rejoined: 'Why, I jest took a simple pleasure, sir, in seeing an amachoor like you talking French about a little thing I painted here in Cedar Street.' For a moment Rosenheim was too indignant to speak, then he burst out with: 'It's an infernal lie; you could no more paint that picture than you could fly.' 'I did paint it, jest the same,' pursued the stranger imperturbably, as Rosenheim, to make an end of the insufferable wag, snapped out sarcastically, 'Perhaps you painted its mate, then, the Bolton Corot.' 'The one that sold for three thousand dollars last week? Of course I painted it; it's the best nymph scene I ever done. Don't get mad, mister; I paint most of the Corots. I'm glad you like 'em.'

"For a moment I feared that little Rosenheim would smite the lank annoyer dead in his tracks. 'For heaven's sake be careful!' I cried. 'The man is drunk or crazy or he may even be right; the paint on this picture isn't two days old.' 'Correct,' declared the stranger. 'I finished it day before yesterday for this sale.' Then a marked change came over Rosenheim's manner. He grew positively deferential. It delighted him to meet an artist of talent; they must know each other better. Cards were exchanged, and Rosenheim read with amazement the grimy inscription '*Campbell Corot, Landscape Artist*.' 'Yes, that's my painting name,' Campbell Corot said modestly; 'and my pictures are almost equally as good as his'n, but not quite. They do for ordinary household purposes. I really hate to see one get into a big sale like the Bolton; it don't seem honest, but I can't help it; nobody'd believe me if I told.' Rosenheim's demeanour was courtly to a fault as he pleaded an engagement and bade us farewell. Already apparently he divined a certain importance in so remarkable a gift of mimicry. I stayed behind, resolved on making the nearer acquaintance of Campbell Corot."

* * * * *

"Rosenheim clearly understands the art of business," interrupted the Antiquary. "And the business of art," added the Critic. "Could your seedy friend have painted my Corot?" said the Patron in real distress. "Why not?" continued the Painter remorselessly. "Only hear me out, and you may judge for yourself. Anyhow, let's drop your Corot; we were speaking of mine."

"To make Campbell Corot's acquaintance proved more difficult than I had expected. He confided to me immediately that he had been a durn fool to give himself away to my friend, but talk was cheap, and people never believed him, anyway. Then gloom descended, and my professions of confidence received only the most surly responses. He unbent again for a moment with, 'Painter feller, you knowed the pesky ways of paint, didn't yer?' but when I followed up this promising lead and claimed him as an associate, he repulsed me with, 'Stuck up, ain't yer? Parley French like your friend? S'pose you've showed in the Saloon at Paris.' Giving it up, I replied simply: 'I have; I'm a landscape painter, too, but I'd like to say before I go that I should be glad to be able to paint a picture like that.' Looking me in the eye and seeing I meant it, 'Shake!' he replied cordially. As we shook, his breath met me fair: it was such a breath as was not uncommon in old - time Cedar Street. Gentlemen who affect this aroma are, I have noticed, seldom indifferent to one sort of invitation, so I ventured hardily: 'You know Nickerson's Glengyle, sir; perhaps you will do me the favour to drink a glass with me while we chat.' Here I could tell you a lot about Nickerson's." "Don't," begged the Critic, who is abstemious. "I will only say, then, that Nickerson's, once an all - night refuge, closes now at three - desecration has made it the yellow marble office of a teetotaler in the banking line - and the Glengyle, that blessed essence of the barley, heather, peat, and mist of Old Scotland, has been taken over by an exporting company, limited. Sometimes I think I detect a little of it in the poisons that the grocers of Glasgow and Edinburgh send over here, or perhaps I only dream of the old taste. Then it was itself, and by the second glass Campbell Corot was quite ready to soliloquise. You shall have his story about as he told it, but abridged a little in view of your tender ages and the hour.

* * * * *

"John Campbell had grown up contentedly on the old farm under Mount Everett until one summer when a landscape painter took board with the family. At first the lad despised the gentle art as unmanly, but as he watched the mysterious processes he longed to try his hand. The good - natured Duesseldorfian willingly lent brushes and bits of millboard upon which John proceeded to make the most lurid confections. The forms of things were, of course, an obstacle to him, as they are to everybody. 'I never could drore,' he told me, 'and I never wanted to drore like that painter chap. Why he'd fill a big canvas with little trees and rocks and ponds till it all seemed no bigger than a Noah's ark show. I used to ask him, "Why don't you wait till evening when you can't see so much to drore?"' To such criticism the painter naturally paid no attention, while John devoted himself to sunsets and the tube of crimson lake. From babyhood he had loved the purple hour, and his results, while without form and void, were apparently not wholly unpleasing, for his master paid him the compliment of using one or two such sketches as backgrounds, adding merely the requisite hills, houses, fences, and cows. These collaborations were mentioned not unworthily beside the sunsets of Kensett and Cropsey next winter at the Academy. From that summer John was for better or worse a painter.

"His first local success was, curiously enough, an historical composition, in which the village hose company, almost swallowed up by the smoke, held in check a conflagration of Vesuvian magnitude. The few visible figures and Smith's turning - mill, which had heroically been saved in part from the flames, were jotted in from photographs. Happily this work, for which the Alert Hose Company subscribed no less than twenty - five dollars, providing also a fifty - dollar frame, fell under the appreciative eye of the insurance adjuster who visited the very ruins depicted. Recognising immediately an uncommonly available form of artistic talent, this gentleman procured John a commission as painter in ordinary to the Vulcan, with orders to come at once to town at excellent wages. By his twentieth year, then, John was established in an attic chamber near the North River with a public that, barring change in the advertising policy of the Vulcan, must inevitably become national. For the lithographers he designed all manner of holocausts; at times he made tours through the counties and fixed the incandescent mouth of Vulcan's forge, the figures within being merely indicated, on the face of a hundred ledges. That was a shame, he freely admitted to me; the rocks looked better without. In fact, John Campbell's first manner soon came to be a humiliation and an intolerable bondage. He felt the insincerity of it deeply. 'You see, it's this way,' he explained to me, 'you don't see the shapes by firelight or at sunset, but you have seen them all day and you know they're there. Nobody that don't have those shapes in his brush can make you feel them in a picture. Everybody puts too little droring into sunsets. Nobody paints good ones, not even Inness [we must remember it was in the early '70s], except a Frenchman called Roosoo. He takes 'em very late, which is best, and he can drore some too.'"

"A very decent critic, your alcoholic friend," the Critic remarked. "He was full of good ideas, as you shall see," the story - teller replied. "I quite agree with you, if the bad whisky could have been kept away from him he might have shone in your profession. Anyhow, he had the makings of an honest man in him, and when the Vulcan enlarged its cliff - painting programme, he cut loose bravely. Then followed ten lean years of odd jobs, with landscape painting as a recreation, and the occasional sale of a canvas on a street corner as a great event. When his need was greatest he consented to earn good wages composing symbolical door designs for the Meteor Coach Company, but that again he could not endure for long. Later in the intervals of colouring photographs, illuminating window-shades, or whatever came to hand, he worked out the theory which finally led him to the feet of Corot. It was, in short, that the proper subject for an artist deficient in linear design is sunrise.

"He explained the matter to me with zest. 'By morning you've half forgotten the look of things. All night you've seen only dreams that don't have any true form, and when the first light comes, nothing shows solid for what it is. The mist uncovers a little here and there, and you wonder what's beneath. It's all guesswork and nothing sure. Take any morning early when I look out of my attic window to the North River. There's nothing but a heap of fog, grey or pink, as there's more or less sun behind. It gets a little thick over toward Jersey, and that may be the shore, or again it mayn't. Then a solid bit of vi'let shows high up, and I guess it's Castle Stevens, but perhaps it ain't. Then a pale-yellow streak shoots across the river farther up and I take it to be the Palisades, but again it may be jest a ray of sunshine. You see there really ain't no earth; it's all air and light. That's what a man that can't drore ought to paint; that's what my namesake, Cameel Corot, did paint better than any one that ever lived.'

"At this point of his confession"At this point of his confession John Campbell glared savagely at me for assent, and set down a sadly frayed and noxious stogy on Nickerson's black walnut. I hastened to agree, though much of the doctrine was heresy to a realist, only objecting: 'But one really has to draw a scene such as you describe just like any other. In fact, the drawing of atmosphere is the most difficult branch of our art. Many very good painters, like my master, Courbet, have given it up.' 'Corbet!' he replied contemptuously; 'he didn't give it up; he never even seen it. But don't I know it's hard, sir? For years I tried to paint it, and I never got nothing but the fog; when I put in more I lost that. They're pretty, those sketches – like watered silk or the scum in the docks with the sun on it; but, Lord, there ain't nothing into 'em, and that's the truth. At last, after fumbling around for years, I happened to walk into Vogler's gallery one day and saw my first Corot. Ther' it was - all I had been trying for. It was the kind of droring I knew ought to be, where a man sets down more what he feels than what he knows. I knew I was beginning too late, but I loved that way of working. I saw all the Corots I could, and began to paint as much as I could his way. I got almost to have his eye, but of course I never got his hand. Nobody could, I guess, not even an educated artist like you, or they'd all a don' it.'

* * * * *

"After this awakening John Campbell began the artist's life afresh with high hopes. His first picture in the sweet new style was honestly called 'Sunrise in Berkshire,' though he had interwoven with his own reminiscences of the farm several motives from various compositions of his great exemplar. He signed the canvas Campbell Corot, in the familiar capital letters, because he didn't want to take all the credit; because he desired to mark emphatically the change in his manner, and because it struck him as a good painting name justified by the resemblance between his surname and the master's Christian name. It was a heartfelt homage in intention. If the disciple had been familiar with Renaissance usages, he would undoubtedly have signed himself John of Camille.

"'Sunrise in Berkshire' fetched sixty dollars in a downtown auction room, the highest price John had ever received; but this was only the beginning of a bewildering rise in values. When John next saw the picture, Campbell had been deftly removed, and the landscape, being favourably noticed in the press, brought seven hundred dollars in an uptown salesroom. John happened on it again in Beilstein's gallery, where the price had risen to thirteen hundred dollars - a tidy sum for a small Corot in those early days. At that figure it fell to a noted collector whose walls it still adorns. Here Campbell Corot's New England conscience asserted itself. He insisted on seeing Beilstein in person and told him the facts. Beilstein treated the visitor as an impostor and showed him the door, taking his address, however, and scornfully bidding him make good his story by painting a similar picture, unsigned. For this, if it was worth anything, the dealer promised he should be liberally paid. Naturally Campbell Corot's professional dander was up, and he produced in a week a Corotish 'Dance of Nymphs,' if anything, more specious than the last. For this Beilstein gave him twenty-five dollars, and within a month you might have seen it under the skylight of a country museum, where it is still reverently explained to successive generations of school-children.

"If Campbell Corot had been a stronger character, he might have made some stand against the fraudulent success his second manner was achieving. But, unhappily, in those experimental years he had acquired an experimental knowledge of the whisky of Cedar Street. His irregular and spend-thrift ways had put him out of all lines of employment. Besides, he was consumed by an artist's desire to create a kind of picture that he could not hope to sell as his own. Nor did the voice of the tempter, Beilstein, fail to make itself heard. He offered an unfailing market for the little canvases at twenty-five and fifty dollars, according to size. There was a patron to supply unlimited colours and stretchers, a pocket that never refused to advance a small bill when thirst or lesser need found Campbell Corot penniless. Almost inevitably he passed from occasional to habitual forgery, consoling himself with the thought that he never signed the pictures and, before the law at least, was blameless. But signed they all were somewhere between their furtive entrance at Beilstein's basement and their appearance on his walls or in the auction rooms. Of course it wasn't the blackguard Beilstein who forged the five magic letters; he would never take the risk, 'Blast his dirty soul!' cried Campbell Corot aloud, as he seethed with the memory of his shame. He rose as if for summary vengeance, to the amazement of the quiet topers in the room. For some time his utterance had been getting both excited and thick, and now I saw with a certain chagrin that the Glengyle had done its work only too well. It was a question not of hearing his story out, but of getting him home before worse befell. By mingled threats and blandishments I got him away from Nickerson's, and after an adventurous passage down Cedar Street, I deposited him before his attic door, in a doubtful frame of mind, being alternately possessed by the desire to send Beilstein to hell and to pray for the eternal welfare of the only genuine Corot."

"You certainly make queer acquaintances," ejaculated the Patron uneasily.

"Hurry up and tell us the rest; it's growing late," insisted the Antiquary, as he beckoned for the bill.

"I saw Campbell Corot only once more, but occasionally I saw his work, and it told a sad tale of deterioration. The sunrises and nymphals no longer deceived anybody, having fallen nearly to the average level of auction-room impressionism. I was not surprised, then, when running into him near Nickerson's one day I felt that drink and poverty were speeding their work. He tried to pass me unrecognised, but I stopped him, and once more the invitation to a nip proved irresistible. My curiosity was keen to learn his attitude toward his own work and that of his master, and I attempted to draw him out with a crass compliment. He denied me gently. 'The best things I do, or rather did, young feller, are jest a little poorer than his worst. Between ourselves, he painted some pretty bum things. Some I suppose he did, like me, by lamplight. Some he sketched with one hand while he was lighting that there long pipe with the other. Sometimes, I guess, he was in a hurry for the money. Now, when I'm painting my level best, like I used to could, mine are about like that. But people don't know the difference about him or about me; and mine, as I told your Jew friend, are plenty good enough for every-day purposes. Used to be, anyway. Nobody can paint like his best. Think of it, young feller, you and me is painters and know what it means - jest a little dirty paint on white canvas, and you see the creeping of the sunrise over the land, the breathing of the mist from the fields, and the twinkling of the dew in the young leaves. Nobody but him could paint that, and I guess he never knowed how he done it; he jest felt it in his brush, it seems to me.'

"After this outburst little more was to be got from him. In a word, he had gone to pieces and knew it. Beilstein had cast him off; the works in the third manner hung heavy in the auction places. Leaning over the table, he asked me, 'Who was the gent that said, "My God, what a genius I had when I done that!"?' I told him that the phrase was given to many, but that I believed Swift was the gent. 'Jest so,' Campbell Corot responded; 'that's the way I felt the last time I saw Beilstein. He'd been sending back my things and, for a joke, I suppose, he wrote me to come up and see a real Corot, and take the measure of the job I was tackling. So up to the avenue I went, and Beilstein first gave me my dressing down and then asked me into the red-plush private room where he takes the big oil and wheat men when they want a little art. There on the easel was a picture. He drew the cloth away and said: "Now, Campbell, that's what we want in our business." As sure as you're born, sir, it was a "Dance of Nymphs" that I done out of photographs eight years ago. But I can't paint like that no more. I know the way your friend Swift felt; only I guess my case is worse than his.'

"The mention of photographs gave me a clue to Campbell Corot's artistic methods. It appeared that Beilstein had kept him in the best reproductions of the master. But on this point the disciple was reticent, evading my questions by a motion to go. 'I'm not for long probably,' he said, as he refused a second glass. 'You've been patient while I've talked - I can't to most - and I don't want you to remember me drunk. Take good care of yourself, and, generally speaking, don't start your whisky till your day's painting is done.' I stood for some minutes on the corner of Broadway as his gaunt form merged into the glow that fell full into Cedar Street from the setting sun. I wondered if the hour recalled the old days on the farm and the formation of his first manner.

"However that may be, his premonition was right enough. The next winter I read one morning that the body of Campbell Corot had been taken from the river at the foot of Cedar Street. It was known that his habits were intemperate, and it was probable that returning from a saloon he had walked past his door and off the dock. His cards declared him to be a landscape painter, but he was unknown in the artistic circles of the city. I wrote to the authorities that he was indeed a landscape painter and that the fact should be recorded on his slab in Potter's Field. I was poor and that was the only service I could do to his memory."

The Painter ceased. We all rose to go and were parting at the doorway with sundry hems and haws when the Patron piped up anxiously, "Do you suppose he painted my Corot?" "I don't know and I don't care," said the Painter shortly. "Damn it, man, can't you see it's a human not a picture-dealing proposition?" sputtered the Antiquary. "That's right," echoed the Critic, as the three locked arms for the stroll downtown, leaving the bewildered Patron to find his way alone to the Park East.

THE DEL PUENTE GIORGIONE

The train swung down a tawny New England river towards Prestonville as I reviewed the stages of a great curiosity. At last I was to see the Del Puente Giorgione. Long before, when the old pictures first began to speak to me, I had learned that the critic Mantovani, the master of us all, owned an early Giorgione, unfinished but of marvellous beauty. At his death, strangely enough, it was not found among his pictures, which were bequeathed as every one knows to the San Marcello Museum. The next word I had of it was when Anitchkoff, Mantovani's disciple and successor, reported it in the Del Puente Castle in the Basque mountains. He added a word on its importance though avowedly knowing it only from a photograph. It appeared that Mantovani in his last days had given the portrait to his old friend the Carlist Marquesa del Puente, in whose cause - picturesque but irrelevant detail - he had once drawn sword. Anitchkoff's full enthusiasm was handsomely recorded after he had made the pilgrimage to the Marquesa's crag. One may still read in that worthy but short-lived organ of sublimity, "Le Mihrab," his appreciation of the Del Puente Giorgione, which he describes as a Giambellino blossoming into a Titian, with just the added exquisiteness that the world has only felt since Big George of Castelfranco took up the brush. How the panel exchanged the Pyrenees for the North Shore passed dimly through my mind as barely worth recalling. It was the usual story of the rich and enterprising American collector. Hanson Brooks had bought it and hung it in "The Curlews," where it bid fair to become legendary once more, but at last had lent it with his other pictures to the Prestonville Museum of Science and the Fine Arts, the goal of my present quest. While the picture lay *perdu* at Brooks's, there had been disquieting gossip; the Pretorian Club, which is often terribly right in such matters, agreed that he had been badly sold. None of this I believed for an instant. What could one doubt in a picture owned by Mantovani and certified by Anitchkoff? Upon this point of rumination the train stopped at Prestonville.

My approach to the masterpiece was reverently deliberate. At the American House I actually lingered over the fried steak and dallied long with the not impossible mince pie. Thus fortified, I followed Main Street to the Museum - one of those depressingly correct new-Greek buildings with which the country is being filled. Skirting with a shiver the bleak casts from the antique in the atrium and mounting an absurdly spacious staircase, I reached a doorway through which the *chefd'oeuvre* of my dreams confronted me cheerlessly. Its nullity was appalling; from afar I felt the physical uneasiness that an equivocal picture will usually produce in a devotee. To approach and study it was a civility I paid not to itself but to its worshipful *provenance*. A slight inspection told all there was to tell. The paint was palpably modern; the surface would not have resisted a pin. In style it was a distant echo of the Giorgione at Berlin. Yet, as I gazed and wondered sadly, I perceived it was not a vulgar forgery - indeed not a forgery at all. It had been done to amuse some painter of antiquarian bent. I even thought, too rashly, that I recognised the touch of the youthful Watts, and I could imagine the studio revel at which he or another had valiantly laid in a Giorgione before the punch, as his contribution to the evening's merriment. The picture upon the pie wrought a black depression that some excellent Japanese paintings were powerless to dispel. As my train crawled up the tawny river, now inky, my thoughts moved helplessly about the dark enigma - How could Mantovani have possessed such rubbish? How could Anitchkoff, enjoying the use of his eyes and mind, have credited it for a moment? My reflections preposterously failed to rest upon the obvious clue, the mysterious Marquesa del Puente, and it was not until I met Anitchkoff, some years later, that I began to divine the woman in the case.

After ten years of absence he had come back to America on something like a triumphal tour. I had promptly paid my respects and now through a discreet persistency was to have a long evening with him at the Pretorian. As I studied the dinner card, guessing at his gastronomic tastes, my mind was naturally on his remarkable career. Anitchkoff, brought from Russia in childhood, had grown up in decent poverty in a small New England city. Very early he showed the intellectual ambition that distinguished all the family. Our excellent public schools made his way to the nearest country college easy and inevitable. There began the struggle the traces of which might be read in an almost melancholy gravity quite unnatural in a man become famous at thirty-five. With the facility of his race he learned all the languages in the curriculum and read ferociously in many literatures. In his junior year the appearance of a great and genial work on psychology made him the metaphysician he has remained through all digressions in the connoisseurship and criticism of art. How his search for ultimate principles involved a mastery of the minutiae of the Venetian school I could only guess. But one could imagine the process. Seeking to ground his personal preferences in a general esthetic, he would have found his data absolutely untrustworthy. How could he presume to interpret a Giorgione or a Titian when what they painted was undetermined? Upon these shifting sands he declined to rear his tabernacle. To the work of classifying the Venetians, accordingly, he set himself with dogged honesty. As a matter of course Mantovani became his chief preceptor - Mantovani who first discovered that the highly complex organism we call a work of art has a morphology as definite as that of a trilobite; that the artist may no more transcend his own forms than a crustacean may become a vertebrate. For a matter of ten years Anitchkoff, espousing a fairly Franciscan poverty, gave himself to this ungrateful task. How he contrived to live in the shadow of the great galleries was a mystery the solution of which one suspected to be bitter and heroic. Gradually recognition as an expert came to him and with it an irksome success. His fame had developed duties, and while his studies in esthetics remained fragmentary, he was persistently consulted on all manner of trivialities. From Piedmont to the confine of Dalmatia he knew every little master that ever made or marred panel or plaster, and he paid the penalty of such knowledge. Surmising the tragedy of his career and its essential nobility I had discounted the ugly rumours connecting him with the sale of the Del Puente Giorgione. When every fool learned that the Giorgione at "The Curlews" was false, many inferred that Anitchkoff, having praised it, must have a hand in Brooks's bad bargain - a conclusion sedulously put about and finally hinted in cold type by certain rival critics. Personally I knew that

Brooks had bagged his find under quite other advice, but while I would always have sworn to Anitchkoff's complete integrity in the whole Del Puente matter, my wonder also grew at so hideous a lapse of judgment. I hopelessly fell back upon such banalities as the errability of mankind, being conscious all the time that some special and most curious infatuation must underlie this particular error. Anitchkoff's card interrupted some such train of thought. He came in quietly as sunshine after fog. His face between the curtains reminded me strangely of the awful moment in the Prestonville Museum - paradoxically, for he was as genuine and reassuring as the Del Puente Giorgione had been baffling and false.

We began dinner with the stiffness of men between whom much is unsaid. As the oystershells departed, however, we had found common memories. He recalled delightfully those little northern towns in the debatable region which from a critic's point of view may be considered Lombard or Venetian, with a tendency to be neither but rather a Transalpine Bavaria. To me also the glow of the Burgundy on the tablecloth brought back strange provincial altarpieces in this territory - marvels in crimson and gold, and a riddle for the connoisseur. Then the talk reached higher latitudes. He mused aloud about that very simple reaction which we call the sense of beauty and have resolutely sophisticated ever since criticism existed - I intent meanwhile and eating most of a mallard as sanguine as a decollation of the Baptist. By the cheese Anitchkoff seemed confident of my sympathy, and I, having found nothing amiss in him except an imperfect enjoyment of the pleasures of the table, was planning how least imprudently might be raised the topic of the Del Puente Giorgione. But it was he who spoke first.

At the coffee he asked me with admirable simplicity what people said about the affair, and I answered with equal candour.

"You too have wondered," he continued.

"Of course, but nothing worse," I replied.

Then with the hesitancy of a man approaching a dire chagrin, and yet with a rueful appreciation of the humour of the predicament that I despair of reproducing, he began:

"It happened about this way. When I first came to Italy and began to meet the friends of Mantovani, they told me of an early Giorgione he owned but rarely showed. He used to speak of it affectionately as 'il mio Zorzi,' to distinguish it perhaps from the more important example he had sold to one of our dilettante iron-masters. The little unfinished portrait I heard of, from those whose opinion is sought, as a superlatively lovely thing. It was mentioned with a certain awe; to have seen it was a distinction. For years I hoped my time would come, but the opportunity was provokingly delayed. How should you feel if Mrs. Warrener should show you all her things but the great Botticelli?" I nodded understandingly. Mrs. Warrener, for a two minutes' delay in an appointment, had debarred me her Whistlers for a year.

"That's the way Mantovani treated me," Anitchkoff continued. "Whenever I dared I asked for the 'Zorzi,' and he always put me off with a smile. That mystified me, for I knew he took a paternal pride in my studies, but I never got any more satisfactory answer from him than that the 'Zorzi' was strong meat for the young; one must grow up to it, like S - and P - and C - (naming some of his closest disciples). These allusions he made repeatedly and with a queer sardonic zest. Occasionally he would volunteer the encouragement - for I had long ago dropped the subject - 'Cheer up, my boy; your turn will come.' When he so Quixotically gave the picture to the Marquesa del Puente, it seemed, though, as if my turn could never come, but I noted that he had been true to his doctrine that the 'Zorzi' was only for the mature; the Del Puente was said to be some years his senior. One knew exasperatingly little about her. It was said vaguely that Mantovani entertained a tender friendship for her, having been her husband's comrade in arms in half a dozen Carlist revolts. That seemed enough to explain the gift."

At this point Anitchkoff must have caught my raised eyebrows, for he added contritely, "It was odd for Mantovani to give away a Giorgione. You're quite right. I was ridiculously young." "You may imagine," he pursued, "that the flight of the Giorgione to the Pyrenees only embittered my curiosity. For years I might have seen it - shabbily to be sure - by merely opening a door when Mantovani was occupied, now it had departed to another planet. Remember those were my 'prentice days when I lived obscurely and absolutely without acquaintance in the Marquesa's world. She seemed as inaccessible as the Grand Lama. But you know how things will come about in least expected ways: Jane Morrison, quite the only human being who could possibly have known both the Marquesa and me, actually gave me a very good letter of introduction. Then almost oppressive good luck, came a note from her mountain Castle, telling that the Chatelaine would be glad to receive me whenever my travels led me her way. She mentioned our common enthusiasm for the Venetians and graciously wanted my opinion on the Giorgione, which the enemies of Mantovani, her friend and my spiritual father, as she called him, had spitefully slandered. Such slanders had never happened to reach my ears but I was already eager to refute them.

"It was two years later that I made the visit on the way to the Prado. All day long the diligence rattled up hill away from the railroad, and it was dusk before I saw the Del Puente stronghold on its crag, evidently a half hour's walk from the miserable *fonda* where the diligence dropped me. It was no hour to present an introduction, but I bribed a boy to take the letter up that night. He returned, disappointingly, without an answer. The next morning wore on intolerably amid a noisy squalor that I could not escape until my summons came. It was early afternoon before an equerry arrived on muleback bearing the Marquesa's note. She was enchanted to meet me but desolated at the unlucky time of my arrival. Tomorrow she crossed the Pyrenees for Paris and hoped my route might lie that way. Meanwhile her home was wholly dismantled for the winter, and the ordinary hospitalities were denied her. But she counted on the pleasure of seeing me at four; we might at least chat, drink a cup of tea, and pay our homage to Mantovani's 'Zorzi.' Nothing could have been more charming or more tantalising. As I toiled up towards the Del Puente barbican I could feel the precious afternoon light dwindling. Breathless I set the castle bell a-jangling with something like despair.

"Heavy doors opened in front of me as I passed the sallyport and the grassgrown courtyard. At the entrance a majordomo in shabby but fairly regal livery greeted me and conducted me through empty corridors and up a massive staircase. The castle was indeed dismantled - apparently had been in that condition from all time. As my superb guide halted before a door which, exceptionally, was curtained, and knocked, my heart failed me. I dreaded meeting this strange noblewoman, almost regretted the nearness of the 'Zorzi,' knowing the actual colours could hardly surpass those of my fancy. The little speeches I had been rehearsing resolved themselves into silence again as I saw her by a tiny fire; a compelling apparition, erect, with snowy hair waving high over burning black eyes. To-day when I coldly analyse her fascination I recall nothing but these simple elements. She permitted not a moment of the shyness that has always plagued me. What our words were I do not now know, but I know that I kissed the two hands she held out to me as she called me Mantovani's son and her friend. Then I talked as never before or since, told her of my struggles and ambitions, and from time to time I was mute so that I might hear the deep contralto of the French she spoke perfectly but with Spanish resonance. There was probably tea. Anyhow the light went away from the deep casements unnoticed, and it was she who, with a chiding finger, recalled me to duty and the Giorgione. 'Wretch,' said she, 'you are here to see it not me. The light is going and your devoirs yet unpaid.'

"As she took my arm and led me through the gallery, I had an odd presentiment of going towards a doom. While I followed her up a winding stair, the misgiving increased. Did venerable lemurs inhabit the Basque mountains? Could so magnificent; an old age be of this earth? An ancestral shudder from the Steppes came over me. It was her ruddy train rustling round the turns ahead that aroused these atavistic superstitions. But when we stood together on the landing all doubts fell away; a broad ray of sunlight that struck through an open doorway showed her spectral beauty to be after all reassuringly corporeal. Over the threshold she fairly pushed me with the warning, 'The place is holy, we must be silent.' For a moment I was staggered by the wide pencil of light that shot through a porthole and cut the room in two. The little octagon, a tower chamber I took it to be, was a prism of shadow enclosing a shaft of flying golddust. Outside it must have been full sunset. Near the border line of light and darkness I faintly saw the 'Zorzi,' which borrowed a glory from the moment and from her. I felt her hand on my shoulder and knelt, it seemed for minutes, it probably was for seconds only. The picture, which I had not seen, much less examined, swam in the twilight and became the most gracious that had ever met my eyes. The dusk grew as the disc of light climbed up the wall and faded. She whispered in my ear, 'It is enough for now. You shall come again many times.' I recall nothing more except the Marquesa's silvery hair and the long line of her crimson gown as she bade me 'Au revoir' at the head of the great stairs. That night in the miserable *fonda* below I wrote out feverishly the notes which you have doubtless read in the 'Mihrab,' and I would give my right hand to be able to forget."

There was a long pause, during which Anitchkoff sipped his cognac nervously, waiting for my comment. I pressed him ruthlessly for the bitter end of the tale.

"Your hypnotism I grant, but what about Mantovani and Brooks?" I asked bluntly.

"For Mantovani I have no right to speak," Anitchkoff replied with dignity. "He was my master and I can admit no imputation on his memory. Besides, your guess is as good as mine. Whether he bought the picture in his precritical days, keeping it as a warning and imposing it upon his followers as a hoax - this I can merely conjecture. As for Brooks, the case is simple; he couldn't resist a Giorgione at a bargain. But since you will, you may as well hear the rest of the story - at least my part of it.

"Three years later I wintered in Paris. I had run into Bing's for a chat and a look at the Hokusais, when who should come in but Hanson Brooks in a high state of elation. An important purchase had just arrived. He urged us both to dine and inspect it. Bing was engaged; I glad to accept. At dinner Brooks teased me to the top of his bent. I was to imagine absolutely the most important old master in private possession, his for a beggarly price. I declined to humour him by guessing, and we slurred his sweets and coffee to hasten to the apartment. On a dressing table faced to the wall was a little panel which he slowly turned into view. For a moment I gasped for joy, it was the Del Puente Giorgione; and then an awful misgiving overcame me - I saw it as it was. Brooks marked my amazement and, misreading the cause, slapped me on the back and asked what I thought of that for a hundred thousand pesetas. The figure again bowled me over. For the picture as it stood it was a thousand times too much, while a mere tithe of the value of the name the panel bore. I blurted out that the price was suspiciously wrong, and added that I must see the portrait by daylight before venturing an opinion. The thought that Mantovani had owned it for twenty years and more made a sleepless night hideous; at sunrise my loyalty reasserted itself by a lame compromise.

"I daresay you will not blame me for hoping against hope, as I did the next day and for some months after, that somewhere under that modern paint there was indeed a sketch by Giorgione's hand. You must remember that I could as little doubt my own existence as Mantovani's judgment on such a point. In the sequel it seemed as if no humiliation were to be spared me. It was Mantovani's chief rival and favourite victim, Merck, who after a torturing correspondence had the pleasure of telling me he had seen the 'Zorzi' painted by the amateur Ricard; it was Campbell who, after recommending it to Brooks, publicly accused me of dishonest brokerage. That's all I can tell you about the Del Puente Giorgione."

I seized his hand impulsively, and clumsily offered him, in a breath, whisky, shuffleboard, or cowboy pool - sound Pretorian remedies for all human woes. These consolations he refused and took his leave. Midnight found me in the same chair, thinking less of Anitchkoff, whose case now lay clear, than of Mantovani and the Marquesa del Puente, about whom it seemed there still might be something to say.

The chances of a roving life have brought some slight addition to the evidence. Stopping over a boat at Dieppe, a few summers ago, I happened to see my good friend Mme. Vezin registered at the Casino, where I recognised an acquaintance or two. That decided me to spend the night and call at her villa. Her salon never failed to divert me, for, drawing together the most disparate people, she handled them with easy generalship. Under her chandelier ardent art students from the Middle West and the poor relations of royalty might be heard exchanging confidences and foreign tongues. So, as I climbed the hill at the verge of the chalk and pasture, I felt sure of the unexpected, nor was I disappointed. Shrill voices from my fellow countrywomen came down the garden path and assured me that art had accompanied Mme. Vezin in her annual retreat from the Luxembourg Gardens. Entering I found the same perfect hostess and much the old dear, queer scene. I was bracing myself for a polyglot evening - being with all my travel quite incapable of languages - when the little maid announced importantly Mme. la Marquise del Puente. All rose instinctively as there entered an erect white-haired woman simply dressed in a black gown along which hung a notable crimson scarf. Murmuring the indispensable banalities I bowed distantly, meaning to observe her impersonally before an encounter. But she disarmed me by throwing herself on my mercy. She knew me already through dear Mr. Hanson Brooks. It was her first visit here; I, she saw, was of the household. Would I not show her the curiosities and protect her from the bores? Sullenly I followed her while she discussed the bijoux that littered the shelves, and the deep modulations of her voice insensibly mollified me. I had intended in Anitchkoff's behalf to count every wrinkle of her seventy-five unhallowed years, but found myself instead admiring her cloud of silver hair, avoiding the gaze of her black eyes, and noting with a kind of fascination the precise gestures of her fine hand as she took up or set down Mme. Vezin's poor little things.

At last she settled into an armchair, beckoning me to a footstool, and I began to talk unconscionably, she urging me on. She professed to know my writings - it was of course impossible that she should have seen those rare anonymous letters to the most ladylike of Boston newspapers: she touched my dearest hobby, that republics and governments generally must be judged not by their politics but by the amenity of the social life they foster. Feeling that this was witchcraft or divination even more questionable, and dreading she had another Giorgione to sell, I made a last futile effort for freedom, proposing introductions. With a phrase she subdued me, and my halting French began to be eloquent. I confessed my innermost ambition, the creation of a criticism learned and judicial in substance but impressionistic in form. She dwelt upon the beauties of her eyrie in the Basque mountains which I must one day see. As we chatted on obliviously an audience of marvelling art students and baigneurs formed about us quietly. Their serried faces suddenly revealed to me my ignominious surrender. I started as from a dream and, as she bade me not forget to call, I kissed her long hand and fled with only a curt farewell to my hostess.

The channel breeze and the scent of the clover sobered me up. My pity went out to Anitchkoff and then I remembered that I had seen Fouquart at the Casino. It seemed too good to be true. Here at Dieppe were both this enigmatic Marquesa and the prime repository of all authentic scandal of our times. For the old dandy Fouquart had lived not wisely but too well through three generations of cosmopolitan gallantry. Had the censorship and his literary parts permitted, he could have written a chronicle of famous ladies that would put the Sieur de Brantome's modest attempt to shame. I found him among the rabble, moodily playing the little horses for five-franc pieces, but at the mention of the Marquesa del Puente he kindled.

"A grand woman," he said emphatically, as he dragged me to a safe corner, "a true model to the anemic and neurotic sex of the day." When asked to specify he told me how the energy and passion of twenty generations of robber noblefolk had flowered in her. Scruples or fears she had never known. From childhood attached to the Carlist cause, she had become the soul of that movement in the Pyrenees. It was she who haggled with British armourers, traced routes, planned commissariats, and most of all drew from far and near soldiers of fortune to captain a hopeless cause. In such recruiting, Fouquart implied, her loyalty had not flinched at the most personal tests. What seemed to mystify Fouquart was that none of these whilom champions ever attained the grace of forgetfulness. Every year many of these tottering old gentlemen still reported at Castle del Puente, and there she held court as of old. He himself, although their relations had been not military but civil, occasionally made so idle a pilgrimage. "To the shrine of our Lady of the crimson teagown," I ventured. "You too, *mon vieux*!" he chuckled with ironical congratulations. Ignoring the impertinence, I interposed the name of Mantovani. "Our respected colleague," Fouquart exclaimed delightedly. Before Mantovani fuddled his head about pictures he had been a good blade, taking anyone's pay. For ten years and through half as many little wars he had been the Marquesa's titular chief of staff. Her husband? Well, her husband was a good Carlist - and a true philosopher. As I tore myself away from the impending flow of scandal, Fouquart murmured regretfully. "Must you go? It is a pity. We have only begun, *a demain*." But we had really ended, for the next morning, shaking off a nightmare of a red-robed Lilith who tried to sell me a questionable Zeuxis, I took the early steamer. Of the Marquesa del Puente, whom I believe to be still at her castle, I have seen or heard nothing since.

* * * * *

After some reflection in the corner of the Pretorian where Anitchkoff once told me his story, I have come measurably into the clear about the whole matter. Mantovani's position is plain up to a certain point. Either the 'Zorzi' was given to him or else he bought it in his hopeful youth. In either case he surely kept it merely as a solemn hoax on his learned contemporaries. He may have withheld it from Anitchkoff maliciously, or again out of simple considerateness for a trusting disciple. When Mantovani came to set his worldly affairs in order, however, it must have struck him that the joke could not be perpetuated on the walls of the San Marcello gallery, while the panel was one that a great connoisseur would not willingly have inventoried by his executors. It was at this time that he bestowed the 'Zorzi' upon the Marquesa del Puente, as a final token between them. It may fairly be assumed that he knew her to be incapable of believing the precious souvenir to be a veritable Giorgione. Such simplicity as that gift and credulity presuppose lay neither in his nature nor in hers. Beyond this point certitudes fail us lamentably, and we are reduced to an exasperating balance of possibilities. Did he send the picture as an elaborate and unavoidable slight? or was it essentially a delicate alms, in view of the Marquesa's known poverty and proved resourcefulness? or, again, did he with a deeper perversity set the thing afloat to trouble the critical world after he was gone, foreseeing perhaps some such international comedy as was actually played with the 'Zorzi' as leading gentleman? All these things must remain problematical for

Mantovani cannot tell, and the Marquesa del Puente will not if indeed she knows.

THE LOMBARD RUNES

Professor Hauptmann dropped wearily into his chair at the noisy Milanese *table d'hote* and snarled out a surly "*Mahlzeit*" to the assembled feasters. It was echoed sweetly from his left with a languishing "*Mahlzeit, Herr Professor*." The advance disconcerted him. Resolving upon a policy of complete indifference to the fluffy and amiable vision beside him, he devoted himself singly to the food. The *risotto* diminished as his knife travelled rhythmically between the plate and his bearded lips. Conceding only the inevitable, nay the exacted courtesies to his neighbour, he performed still greater prodigies with the green peas, and it was not until he leaned back for a deft operation with a pocket comb, that the vivacious, blue-eyed one got her chance to ask if it were not the Herr Professor Hauptmann, the great authority on the Lombard tongue. The query floored him; he could not deny that it was, and as curlylocks began to evince an intelligent interest in Lombard matters, his stiffness melted like wax under a burning glass. He was soon if not the protagonist at least the object of an animated, yes fairly intimate conversation.

To non-German eyes the pair were worth looking at. He was clad in tightfitting sage-green felt, so it appeared, with a superfluity of straps, buttons, lacings, and harness of all sorts. A conical Tyrol hat garnished with a cock's plume and faded violets was crushed between his back and that of the chair. As his large nervous feet reached for the chairlegs below, one could see an expanse of moss-green stockings, only half concealed at the extremities by resplendent yellow sandals. Bearded and moustached after the military fashion, nothing betrayed the professor except the myopic droop of the head. As for Frauelein Linda Goeritz, no mere man may adequately describe her. A German new woman of the artistic stamp, she was pastelling through Lombardy where the Professor was archeologising. Short, crisp curls gathered about her boyish head. Her general effect was of a plump bonniness that might yield agreeably to an audacious arm. She cultivated an aggressive pertness that would have seemed vulgar, had it not been redeemed by something merely frank and German. Shortskirted, she wore a high-strapped variant of the prevalent sandals. The sides of her blue bolero were adorned with stilted yellow lilies in the top of the Viennese new-art mode. In front her shirtwaist appeared cool and white, at the sleeves it flowered alarmingly into something like an India shawl. A string of massive amethysts completed a discord as elaborate as a harmony of Richard Strauss. Her whole impression was almost as inviting as it was grotesque. One could not chat with her without liking her, and it is to be suspected that only a very guileless or austere male could like her without proceeding to manifest attentions.

By the cheese, she had captured her amazed professor, and then she carried him off bodily for coffee in the Arcade. He talked little, but it didn't matter, for she talked much and well. Nor could a provincial Saxon scholar be quite indifferent at finding himself known to an intelligent and much travelled Viennese. A cousin, it appeared, had followed his lectures and had highly extolled the ingenuity of his phonology of the Lombard tongue, a language which was, she must remember - a hesitating pause - yes, surely East - "East Germanic, Ja wohl!" responded the Professor thunder-rously, though idiots had written to the contrary. And then he told her at length the reasons why, until she pleaded her early morning sketching and firmly bound him to accompany her the next afternoon to the Certosa of Pavia. The Herr Professor rarely paid much attention to hands, but as he held Frauelein Goeritz's for Good Night he could not but note that it was soft and filled his big grip so well that he was sorry when it was gone. He dismissed the observation, however, as unworthy a philologer and went to sleep pondering a new destruction for the knaves who held the Lombard tongue to be not East but West Germanic.

And here, to appreciate the weight and importance of Linda's fish, a little explanation is necessary. Hauptmann was not merely a philologer, which is a formidable thing in itself, but he belonged to the esoteric group that deals with languages which have no literature. As he had often remarked, any fool could compile a grammar of a language that has left extensive documents; the process was almost mechanical, but to reconstruct a grammar of a language that has left practically no remains, that required acumen. Hauptmann did not belong, however, to the transcend-dental school that creates purely inferential languages - East Germanic and West, General Teutonic, Original Slavic, Indo-European and the like. These are the *Dii majores* and their inventions are as complete as if one should detect, say, the relation of the little to the big fleas not by the cunning use of the microscope but by sheer inference. This larger game Hauptmann sagaciously left to others, ranging himself with those who piece together the scanty and uncertain fragments of languages that have existed but have failed to perpetuate themselves in documents and inscriptions. Vandalic had powerfully allured him, and so had Old Burgundian: he had had designs also upon Visigothic, and had finally chosen Lombard rather than the others because the material was not merely defective but also delightfully vague, affording a wide opportunity for genuine philological insight. And indeed to classify a language on the basis of a phrase scratched on a brooch, the misquotations of alien chroniclers, the shifting forms of misspelled proper names, is a task compared with which the fabled reconstruction of leviathan from a single bone is mere child's play.

From the mere scraps and hints of Lombard words in Paul the Deacon and other historians anybody but a German would have declined to draw any conclusion whatever. But just as every German citizen however humble, becomes eventually a privy counsellor, a knight of various eagles of diverse classes, an over-stationmaster, or a royal postman, so German science for the past hundred years has permitted no fact to languish in its native insignificance. All have been promoted to be the sponsors of imposing theories. And Hauptmann's theory, which got him the degree of Ph.D., *maxima cum laude*, was that Lombard is an East Germanic tongue. This he simple intuited, needing the degree, for the fifty mangled Lombard words displayed none of those consonants which tending to double or of those vowels which still vexing us as umlauts, mark a language as belonging to the great Eastern or Western group. But Hauptmann was first in the field, and if it was impossible for him to demonstrate that he was right, it was equally impossible for anybody else to prove that he was wrong. So he stood his ground and by dint of continually hitting the same nail on the same head he had so greatly flourished that he was mentioned respectfully as far as the Lombard tongue was known, and at thirty-four had passed from the honourable but unpaid condition of Privat-dozent to that of Professor Extraordinarius.

Now if the Lombards, having ignominiously taken to Latin after their descent upon Italy, had had to wait for Hauptmann to provide them with a language, they had left certain more substantial traces of themselves in the valley of the Po. They died and were buried in state with their arms and utensils for the other world. So that, while one might well be in doubt whether an inscription was Lombard or not, an antiquary will tell you without fail whether a clasp, a spearhead or a sword is or is not the work of this conquering but too adaptable race. In these archaeological matters Hauptmann took a forced and languid interest. During nightmarish hours, when the beer and cheese had not mingled aright, he was haunted by lines of Lombard runes. Sometimes they were East Germanic, and that was a grief, taking, as it were, the bloom from the guess that had made him great; and again they were West Germanic, and that was awful, the hallucination ending in a mortal struggle with the feather bed under which German science is incubated, and passing off with an anguished "Donnerwetter! It cannot be Lombard. It is not possible." His not infrequent Italian trips had, then, an archaeological pretext, and this had been more or less the purpose of the pilgrimage in which Frauelein Linda had become by main force an alluring if disquieting incident.

If there is anywhere in the world a more satisfactory

sight than the Pavian Certosa, certainly neither Hauptmann nor his chance acquaintance had ever seen it. And indeed is there anywhere else such spaciousness of cloisters, such profusion of minutely cut marble, such incrustation, for better or worse, of semiprecious stones. Surely nothing in a sightseeing way approaches it as a money's worth. Frauelein Linda, a superior person who had begun to entertain doubts as to the externals of modern Austrian palaces and the internals of new German liners, reserved her enthusiasms for the pale Borgonones so strangely misplaced amid all that splendour. Hauptmann, on the contrary, admired it all impartially. The sense of bulk and inordinate expensiveness made him for a moment almost regret that these later Lombards who reared this pile were not of the same race-stock with himself. There was a moment in which he could have claimed them, had principle permitted, as West Germans. Rather he soon forgot the Lombards in the alternate rapture and dismay aroused by the petulant yet strangely winning personality beside him. Professor Hauptmann was used neither to being contradicted nor managed by mere women folk, and this afternoon he was undergoing both experiences simultaneously. It was with a feeling of relief that he left the Certosa, which seemed in a way her territory, and started out with her upon the neutral highroad that led to the station. They lingered, for the hour was propitious, and their plan was to kill an hour or so before the evening train. As the glow came over the lowlying fields, the weary forms of the labourers began to fill the road. At a distance Hauptmann perceived one who importunately offered a small object to the sightseers and was as regularly repulsed. Without waiting for the professor, who stood at attention while Frauelein Linda sketched, this beggar or pedlar approached and prayed to be allowed to show a rare and veritable object of antiquity. A gruff refusal had already been given when she pleaded that they hear the peasant talk, and inspect his treasure. "Who knows, Herr Professor, but it might be Lombard?" "Wohlan," he replied, and sullenly took the proffered spearhead. It was of iron, patined rather than rusted, Lombard in form, and of evident antiquity. Hauptmann gave it a nearsighted look and was about to return it contemptuously when the peasant urged, "But look again, sir, there are letters, a rarity." "I dare you to read them," cried Frauelein Linda, and the Professor read painfully and copied roughly in his notebook a short inscription in some Runic alphabet. A scowl followed the reading and the abrupt challenge "Where did you find this piece?" "In the fields, digging, Padrone," was the answer, "where I dug up also this," displaying a bronze clasp of unquestionable Lombard workmanship. "Bravo," exclaimed Linda, "now perhaps we shall know more about your dear Lombards. I congratulate you, Herr Professor, from the heart." "Aber nein," he growled back, "there were monuments enough already, and this is only a bore, for I must buy and publish it. Others too may be found in the same field, and Lombard will become a popular pastime. It is disgusting; compassionate me. It was the single language that permitted truly a-priori approach. It would be almost a duty to suppress these accursed runes for the sake of scientific method. But no; the harm is done. We must be patient."

What the Herr Professor said and continued to say as he drove a hard bargain with the peasant was but half the story. A glance at the runes had shown an awful double consonant, and, as if that were not enough, an appalling modified vowel. By a single word scratched by the untutored hand of a rude warrior the most ingenious linguistic hypothesis of our times was shattered beyond hope of repair. The spearhead was Lombard, and Lombard, dire reflection to one who had gained fame by maintaining the contrary, belonged to the West Germanic group of the Teutonic tongues. Wild thoughts went through his head. He recalled that Paris had seemed worth a mass, and considered a plenary retraction with a facsimile publication of the runes. But as he pondered this course the inexpediency of sacrificing so fair a theory to this mere brute fact seemed indisputable. He thought also of ascribing the doubled consonant and the modified vowel to the illiterate blundering of the spearman who chiselled the letters. But as his fingers traced the sharp and purposeful strokes he realised that such a contention would be laughed out of the philological court. For a mad moment he thought of destroying the miserable bit of iron, but in the first place that was in itself difficult, and then the chattering lady at his side knew that he was in possession of a Runic inscription, probably Lombard. She was widely connected and would certainly babble in the very city where his bitter rival Professor Anlaut had maintained that Lombard was West Germanic. As Hauptmann noticed that the road had become deserted, that the dusk had increased, and that Frauelein Linda's observations on the luckiness of the "find" were interminable, a homicidal fancy just grazed the border of his agitated consciousness. But no, that would not do either; the scientific conscience forbade the destruction of any datum however embarrassing. Destroy the spearhead he could not, and with a flash of intuition it came over him that it must simply be lost as promptly and hopelessly as possible.

But this too was by no means easy. As they strolled

down the road, ditch after ditch in the lower fields presented itself as apt for the purpose, but never the favourable moment. In fact Frauelein Linda's talk came back to the accursed runes with exasperating persistency. They would confirm his theory. She was happy in being present at this auspicious discovery. It would be a cause wherefore she should not wholly be forgotten. It was this sentimental hint that gave a reasonable hope of taking her mind off the runes, and the harassed philologer set himself resolutely to the task. For her slight advances he found bolder responses, and still scanning the irrigating ditches closely for an especially oozy bottom, he expatiated on the loveliness of the afterglow and confirmed the recollection of last evening that Frauelein Linda's dimpled hand might be an eminently pleasant thing to hold. Thus gradually she was won from the Lombard runes to more personal interests, and as in the slow progress towards the station they neared a bridge, Hauptmann divined the spot where the East Germanic hypothesis lately in peril of death might receive an indefinite reprieve.

He found Linda, as he now called her, neither disinclined to sit on the parapet nor to receive the support of his arm. Her chatter had dwindled to sighs and exclamations. He felt the need of a competing sound as the chug of the spearhead in the ditch should announce the discomfiture of the West Germans. But before committing the telltale runes to this ditch, Hauptmann scanned it carefully over Linda's curly head, and considered thoughtfully its worthiness to receive so important a deposit. The survey could not have been more reassuring. Like so many of the main irrigating ditches that carry the water of Father Po and his tributaries to the lower fields, the sluggish stream consisted equally of water, weeds, and ooze. No Lombard or other object held in that mixture was likely soon to be found. There was a moment of tense silence and then a single plucking sound which various eavesdroppers might have located at the surface of the ditch or near Linda's plump left cheek. Neither guess would have been wrong, for if she sighed once more it was not for the vanishing Lombard runes.

Frauelein Linda Goeritz is, if something of a sentimentalist, also a bit of an analyst, and when, in the train, she learned that the spearhead was lost she accepted Hauptmann's cheerful comment with a certain scepticism. He insisted with a suspicious vivacity that it didn't matter, that indeed he preferred to have the merely professional reminiscence eliminated from an experience that had personally moved him so deeply. To this reading of the affair she naturally could not object, but as she gave him her hand quite formally for farewell, she said: "To-night you have forgotten the runes, tomorrow you forget me, nicht wahr? You are wrong. Them you will not find again: there are many of me. You should have forgotten me first." She escaped while a protest was on his lips.

Since that evening Frauelein Goeritz has followed Professor Hauptmann's brilliant career with a certain interest and perplexity. He has ceased to be an Extraordinarius, but his promotion was based on his ingenious researches in Vandalic. After that trip to the Certosa he discontinued all Lombard studies, and, it is said, actually withdrew from publication a scathing article in which the West Germanic contingent were handled according to their deserts. She has a vague and not wholly comfortable feeling of having counted for something as a deterrent, and she has been heard to hint that his strange distaste for his favourite Lombard investigations, is due to a deep and intimates cause - an unfortunate affair of the heart associated with that historic region.

THEIR CROSS

How their cross reached Fourth Avenue one may only surmise, but there surely was knavery at some point of its transit. It was too splendid in its enamelling, too subtle in the chiselling of its gilded silver to have slipped into the byways of the antiquary's trade with the consent of the Tuscan bishop who controlled or should have controlled its sale. For the matter of that, it still contained one of St. Lucy's knuckles, which in case of a regular transaction would have been transferred to a less precious reliquary. No, there must have been a pilfering sacristan, or worse, a faithless priest, to explain its translation from the Chianti hills to Novelli's shop in Fourth Avenue.

Once there it was certain that one day or another John Baxter must find it. How he became infected with the collector's greed and acquired the occult knowledge that feeds that malady it would take too long to tell. Yet it may be said that the yearning amateur was about the only potent ingredient in the mild composite that was John Baxter. His eyes, skin, hair, and raiment had never seemed of any particular colour, nor did he as a whole seem of any especial size. His parents, who were neither rich nor poor, cultured nor the contrary, had sent him to an indifferent school and college. In the latter he had joined a middling chapter of a poorish fraternity, and, was graduated with a rank that was neither high nor low. During those four easy going years he had played halfhearted baseball and football, and had all but made the "Literary Monthly."

On entering the world, as the phrase goes, he came into possession of a small patrimony and accepted a minor editorial position on a feeble religious monthly. For the ensuing fifteen years John Baxter overtly read manuscripts, composed headlines for edifying extracts, even wrote didactic little articles on his own account. Secretly, meanwhile, the lust of the eye was claiming him, and he was becoming surcharged with a single great passion.

His ascent through books, prints, Colonial furniture, miniatures, rugs, and European porcelain to the dizzy heights of Chinese porcelain and Japanese pottery and painting, it would be tedious and unprofitable to follow. It is enough to say that all along the course his dull grey eye emphatically proved itself the one thing not mediocre about him. It grasped the quality of a fine thing unerringly; it sensed a stray good porcelain from the back row of the auction room. How he knew without knowing why was a mystery to his fellows and even to himself. For if he frequented the museums of New York, and had made one memorable pilgrimage to the Oriental collections of Boston, he was quite without travel, and his education had been chiefly that of the shops and salesrooms. Thus his finds represented less knowledge than an active faith which served as well. A Gubbio lustre jug of museum rank had been bought before he knew the definition of majolica. Before he had learned the peril of such a hazard he had fearlessly rescued a real Kirman mat from an omnibus sale. His scraps of old Chinese bronze and stoneware represented the promptings of a demon who had yet to discover the difference between Sung and Yungching.

These achievements gave John Baxter a certain notoriety in his world and the unusual luxury of self esteem. What brought him the scorn of blunter associates, who openly derided him as a crank, assured him a certain deference from the *cognoscenti*. The small dealers respected him as an authority; the auctioneers greeted him by name as he slipped into his chair, and appealed to him personally when a fine lot hung shamefully. He had the entree at two or three of the more discerning among the great dealers, who occasionally asked his opinion or gave him a bargain. In short a really impressive John as he sees himself was growing up within the skin of poor John Baxter, feeble scribbler for the weak-kneed religious press. As he looked about his cluttered room of an evening he could whisper proudly, "No, it's not a collection, but I can wait. And there is meanwhile nothing in this room that is not good, very good of its type." Sometimes in more expansive musings he would take out of its brocaded bag a wooden tobacco box artfully incrusted with lacquer, pewter, and mother of pearl, the work of the great Korin, and would declare aloud, "Nobody has anything better than this, no museum, certainly no mere millionaire."

Such days and nights had fed an already inordinate craving. He burned for the beautiful things just beyond his grasp, suffered for them amid his morning moralisings, dreamt of them at night. His was never the disinterested love of the beautiful that certain lucky collectors retain through all the sordidness of the quest. Had you observed John in the auction room you would have felt something concentratedly feline in his attitude and would hardly have been surprised had he pounced bodily upon a fine object as it passed near him down the aisle. No other ghost of the auction rooms - and strange enthusiasts they are, had an eye that gleamed with so ominous a fire. There is peril in turning even a weak will into a narrow channel. It may exert amazing pressures - like the slender column of mere water that lifts a loaded car to, or with bad direction, through, the roof.

* * * * *

Whether we should call John Baxter's courtship and marriage a digression or the culmination of his career as a collector might have remained doubtful were it not for the cross in Fourth Avenue. When he found it, hardly a week before he met Miriam Trent, he naturally did not take it for a touchstone. That it was in a manner such, may be inferred from the fact that the anxious morning before the wedding, he stopped at Novelli's for a last look, a ceremony strangely parodying the bachelor supper of more ordinary bridegrooms. After a lingering survey of its deep translucent enamels penned within crisply chiselled silver, like tiny lakes rimmed by ledges, he handed the cross back to the reverent Novelli. It had never looked more desirable, he barely heard Novelli's genial congratulation on the coming of the great day, as he wondered how so splendid a rarity had stayed in that little shop for two years. On reflection the reason was simple. The price, six hundred dollars, was a shade high for another dealer to pay, while the cross itself was so fine an object as merely to excite the distrust of Novelli's average customers. "Fools," muttered John, "how little they know," and hurried towards the florist's. As he made his way back towards an impressive frock-coat, his first, he found himself recalling with a certain satisfaction that even if this were not his wedding day, he really never could have hoped to buy the cross.

What Miriam Trent would have thought had she learned that her bridegroom waived all comparison between herself and the cross only because it was unattainable, one may hardly surmise. But as a sensible person who already knew John's foible and was accustomed to making allowances, she possibly would have been amused and just a bit relieved. She was everything that he was not. Where one passion absorbed him, she gave herself gladly to many interests and duties. A second mother to her numerous small brothers and sisters, and to her amiable inefficient father as well, she had somehow managed school and college for herself, and in accepting John and his worldly goods she gave up a decently paid library position. The insides of books were also familiar to her, in impersonal concerns she had a shrewd sense of people, in general she faced the world with a brave and delicate assurance. Finally she believed with fervour the creed and ethics that John happened to inculcate every week, and it is to be feared that she took him for a prophet of righteousness. Armed at all points that did not involve her personal interests, there was she peculiarly vulnerable. She must have accepted John, aside from the glamour of his edifying articles, simply because of his evident and plaintively reasserted need of her.

Yet they were very happy together, as people who marry on this unequal basis often are. After their panoramic week at Niagara, along the St. Lawrence, and home by the two lakes and the Hudson, they settled down in John's room, which by the addition of two more had been promoted to being the living room of an apartment. Her few personal possessions made a timid, tolerated appearance between his gilt Buddhas and pewter jugs. But she herself queened it easily over the bizarre possessions now become hers. Had you seen her of an evening, alert, fragile, golden under the lamp, and had you seen John's vague glance turn from a moongrey row of Korean bowls to her deeper eyes, you would have been convinced not merely that he regarded her as the finest object in his collection, but also that he was right. It would be intrusive to dwell upon the joys and sorrows of light housekeeping in New York on a small income. Enough to say that the joys preponderated in this case. They read much together, he gradually cultivated an awkward acquaintance with her friends - he had practically none, and at times she made the rounds of the curiosity shops and auctions with him. Here, she explained, her part was that of discourager of enthusiasm, but repression was never practised in a more sympathetic and discerning spirit. Her taste became hardly inferior to his, and their barren quests together established a new comradeship between them. It was probably, then, merely an accident that he never included Novelli's in these aimless rounds, and so never showed her the enamelled cross.

In the long run their imaginary foraging, always a recreation to her, became a sore trial to him. With the demonstration that two really cannot live cheaper than one, the old covetousness smouldering for want of an outlet once more burned hotly within. It expressed itself outwardly in a general uneasiness and irritability. The little fund, her money and his, that lay in savings bank began to spend itself fantastically. One day he reckoned that two-thirds of the cross had been put by, and banished the disloyal thought with difficulty. Visionary plans of selling something and making the collection pay for itself were entertained, but when it came to the point nothing could be spared. Perhaps the gnawings of this hunger might have been controlled, had he thought to confide in Miriam. More likely yet, a system of rare and strictly limited indulgence might have banked the fires between times. However that be, the thwarted collector was to be sunk for a time in the devoted husband. Miriam lay ill of a wasting fever.

After a two days' trial of the rooms, the doctor and the trained nurse, who scornfully slept amid the collection, regarding it as a permanent centre of infection, declared the situation impossible, and with the slightest preliminary consultation of bewildered John, white-coated men were sent for, who carried Miriam to the hospital. About her door John hung like a miserable debarred ghost, for after the first few days her mind wandered painfully, and his presence excited her dangerously. For weeks he vacillated between perfunctory work at the office, unsatisfactory talks with busy doctors and impatient nurses, and long apprehensive hours in what had been home. In "Little Venice," in the best powder-blue jar and the rest, he found no solace, on the contrary, the occasion of revolting suggestions. There was an imp that whispered that she must die and that he should resume collecting. With horror he fled the evil place, and spent an endless night on tolerance within hearing of her moanings.

Fevers have this of merciful, that a term is set for them. Her malady though it often maims cruelly rarely kills. The temperature line on the chart, which for days had described a Himalaya, dwindled suddenly to a Sierra, as quickly to an Appalachian, and then became a level plain. Terribly wracked by the ordeal but safe they pronounced her. The visiting physician occasionally omitted her in his daily round. But convalescence was more trying than the struggle with the fever. The lethargic hours seldom brought either sleep or rest. Beset by nervous fears, the collective suffering of the giant building weighed upon her, and she begged to be taken home.

It was a pathetic triumphal entry that she made among their household gods. The sheer grotesqueness of her home struck her painfully for the first time, as she was helped to an ancient chair that stood before the suspended Kirman rug - her throne John had always called it. As she once more occupied it, there came a curious revulsion against her gorgeously shabby domain. Other women, she reflected, had neat places, cool expanses of wallpaper, furniture seemly set apart. She resented the stuffiness of it all, the air of musty preciousness that pervaded the room. And when John took both her hands and said: "Now the collection is itself again; the queen has come home," she broke down and cried. She did much of that in the weeks that followed. You would have supposed her another person than plucky Miriam Baxter. But the situation hardly made for cheerfulness. Light housekeeping being no longer practicable, they depended on the unwilling ministrations of a slovenly maid. John, who, to do him justice, had never boasted much surplus vitality, felt vaguely that something was now due from him that he could not supply. To escape an inadequacy that was painful he drifted back to the exhibitions and sales, this time alone. He never bought anything, for he was saving manfully for a purpose that daily increased in his mind. He would pay with his pocketbook what with his person he could not.

His always modest luncheon reduced itself to a sandwich, he walked to save carfares, cut off two Sunday newspapers, wore a threadbare spring overcoat into the winter. Then one day he took Miriam to a famous specialist from whom they learned very much what they already knew, but with the advantage of working orders. The great man told John in brief that it was a bad recovery which might readily become worse. A change and open air life were imperative; a sea voyage would be best. If such a change were not made, and soon, he would not be answerable for the consequences.

All this John retold in softened form to Miriam in the waiting room. "We might as well give it up," she said resignedly. "Of course we can't travel. We haven't the money, and you can't get away." With the nearest approach to pride he had ever shown in a nonaesthetic matter John protested that he could get away, and better yet that there was money, five hundred good dollars, more than enough for a glimpse at the Azores and Gibraltar, a hint of rocky Sardinia, a day at Naples, a quiet fortnight on the sunny Genoese Riviera, and then home again by the long sea route. His thin voice rose as he pictured the voyage. Even she caught something of his spirits, and as they got off the car near Novelli's, by a sudden inspiration John said, "Now for being a good girl, and doing what the doctor says, you shall see the most beautiful thing in New York."

In a minute Novelli was carefully taking the precious thing from its drawer and solemnly unfolding the square of ruby velvet in which it lay. Miriam saw the rigid Christ, at the left Mary Mother in azure enamel, at the right the Beloved Apostle in Crimson. From the top God Father sent down the pearly dove through the blue. Below, a stately pelican offered its bleeding breast to the eager bills of its young. And it all glowed translucently within its sharp Gothic mouldings. Behind, the design was simpler - in enamelled discs the symbols of the evangelists. St. Lucy's knuckle lay visible under a crystal lens at the crossing, and surely relic of a saint was seldom encased more splendidly. Even pathetic Miriam kindled to it. "Yes, it is the most beautiful thing in New York," she admitted. "I suppose it costs a fortune, Mr. Novelli." "No, a mere nothing, for it, six hundred dollars." "Why, we might almost buy it," she cried. "It's lucky you haven't saved more, John. I really believe you would buy it." "I'd like to sell it to Mr. Baxter," said Novelli, "he understands it," only to be cut short with a brusque, "No, it's out of our class, but I wanted Mrs. Baxter to see it, and I wanted you to know that she appreciates a fine object as much as I do." "Evidently," said Novelli as they parted. "I hope she will do me the honour of coming in often; there are few who understand, and whether they buy or not I am always glad to have them in my place."

About a week later John Baxter closed and locked his office desk, hurried down to the savings bank, and drew five hundred dollars. Most of it was to go into steamer tickets forthwith, a little balance was to be changed into Italian money. As he meditated a route downtown, he recalled the only adieu still left unpaid. To be sure the cross had remained for three years at Novelli's but it might go forever any day, and with it a great resource for a weary moralist. Farewells were plainly in order, and with no other thought he walked back to the shop and greeted Novelli, who without waiting to be asked produced the crimson parcel that contained the precious relic. As John looked it over from panel to panel, as if to stamp every composition upon his memory, Novelli watched him, reflected, hesitated, smiled benevolently, and spoke. "Mr. Baxter, I am in great need of money and must sacrifice the cross. I want you to take it. Vogelstein has offered me four hundred and fifty dollars for it but he shall not have it if I can sell it to anybody who deserves it better and will value it. It is yours at that price. What do you say?"

John tried for words that failed to come.

"It's a bargain, Mr. Baxter," pursued Novelli, "but of course if you don't happen to have the money there's nothing more to say."

"But I have it right here," retorted John in perplexity, "only it's for quite a different purpose."

"You know your own business, of course, and I don't urge you, but if you have the money and don't take it, you make a great mistake. You know that well enough, and then remember how Mrs. Baxter admired it the other day."

"Yes-s," faltered John dubiously.

"Then why do you hesitate? You know what it is, and what it is worth, as an investment, I mean. By taking your time and selling it right you can surely double your money."

"But" -

"No, there it is. I am honestly doing you a favour," and Novelli thrust the swathed cross into the hands of his fairly hypnotised customer. John's left hand clutched it instinctively, while with the frightened fingers of his right he counted off nine fifty dollar bills.

"Thank you, Mr. Baxter, neither you nor your wife will ever regret it. Nobody in America has anything finer, and that you know."

These words pounded terribly in John's brain as he found his way home, stumbled up stairs, and boggled with the latchkey. All the way down, unheeded passersby had wondered at the crimson burden (he had not waited for a parcel to be made) hugged closely to the shabby black cutaway. The danger signal smote Miriam in the eyes as she rose to be kissed. Standing away from her, he placed the shrouded cross on the table and tried for the confession that would not say itself.

"Why, it's our cross," she cried wonderingly. "Mr. Novelli has lent it to us for a last look before we go where the lovely thing was made. But, John, what's the matter? How you do look! Has something awful happened?"

"Yes," and the pale nondescript head sunk into his hands. "I have bought it. I don't know how. I had the money, I was there, and I bought it."

She repressed the word that was on her lips, and the harder thought that was in her mind, looked long at his humiliation until the pity of a mother came over her tired face. She had mercifully escaped scorning him. Then she spoke.

"It was a bad time to buy it, wasn't it, Dear, but it is a beautiful thing, almost worth a real trip to Italy." She added with a curious air of a suppliant, "And then perhaps we can sell it."

"Yes, that's so, perhaps we can sell it," echoed John listlessly, wrapping the cross closely in its crimson cover and laying it in his most treasured lacquer box. "Yes, perhaps we can sell it," he repeated, and there was a long silence between them.

THE MISSING ST. MICHAEL

Dennis, our Epicurean sage, addressed us all as we lolled on his terrace, drank his tea, and divided our attention between his fluent wisdom and his spacious view of the Valdarno.

"The question is," he repeated, "what will Emma do? Will she be brave, or, rather ordinary enough, to act for herself and him, or will she refuse him because of what she thinks we shall think of them both? As we calmly sit here she may be deciding. That is if you are sure, Harwood, that Crocker was really bound for Emma's when you saw him."

"How could anybody mistake his beaming Emma face?" growled Harwood. "He was marching like a squad of Bersaglieri." "And she knows that Crocker wants it terribly?" added the Sage's wife.

"She does, indeed," sighed Frau Stern repentantly, "for that demon (pointing to Harwood) did tell me and I haf, babylike, told her."

"Here is the case, then," resumed Dennis: "She knows we know Crocker wants her and it, but she doesn't know he doesn't know she has it."

"Precisely, most clearly and gracefully put, my dear,"

laughed Mrs. Dennis.

"And she knows, too," he pursued imperturbably, "that we may think he wants her merely for it."

"Bravo!" puffed Harwood smokily from his camp-stool. "She is too clever to expect any weak generosity from any of us. She believes we will think the worst. And won't we? Viva Nietzsche, and perish pity!"

"Shame upon us, then," cried Frau Stern. "She will gif up that fine young man for fear of our talk? Never!"

"She will send him away, dear Frau Stern, the moment he gives her the chance," declared Dennis. "What else can she do? She can never take the chance of our surmises. Behold us, the destroyers! The victims are prepared."

"Can't we do something about it?" Harwood chuckled. "Repent? Be as harmless as doves? Let's write a roundrobin solemnly stating that, to the best of our knowledge and belief, he wants her for herself and not for it."

"Gently," exclaimed Mrs. Dennis, as she blew out Harwood's poised and lighted match. "You surely don't imagine Crocker will propose the very day she shows it to him."

"My dear," protested Dennis, "don't we all know him well enough to understand that any shock will produce that effect? If his mother died or his horse, his vines got the scale, his Ghirlandaio sprung a crack, his university gave him an honorary degree - these would all be reasons for proposing to Emma. Dear old

Crocker is like that; any jolt would affect him that way."

"Has it occurred to anybody that Emma may have foreseen just this complication and quietly got rid of it first?" suggested Mrs. Dennis, the really practical member of our group, adding, "That's how I'd have served you if I'd wanted him."

"Never," responded Dennis. "She loves it too well, and then she would feel we felt she had spirited it away on purpose."

"Besides," continued Harwood, whose buried aspirations Emmawards had long ago flowered into a minute analysis of her moods, "she is true blue, you know. She will never serve us like that. She may immolate the mighty Crocker upon the altar of our collective curiosity, but she will never dodge us."

"Cannot we all go back to our own countries and leave them alone," suggested Frau Stern almost tearfully; "but no; we no longer haf countries. Here we belong; elsewhere the air is too strong for our little lungs. I pity us, and I pity more those poor young people. If only they will but haf the sense to trample on our talk."

"That, too, would be a sensation," Dennis added cheerfully, and we went our ways, as usual, without having reached anything so vulgar as a conclusion.

* * * * *

Meanwhile Emma Verplanck stood in the _loggia_ of her tiny villa and winced in the focus of the curiosities she despised. She scanned the white road that rimmed her valley before descending sharply to Florence beyond the hill, and especially the crescent of dust where an approaching figure would first appear. Now and then, as if for a rest, her eye traced the line of flaming willows down toward the plunge of her brook into the larger valley, or the file of spectral poplars that led into the vineyards hanging on the declivity of Fiesole. Above all, the gaunt and gashed bulk of Monte Ceceri glistened hotly against a pale blue sky, for if it was a backward April, the first stirring of summer was already in the air. She thrilled with disgust as she asked herself why she dreaded this call. Why should she fear lest an elementary test, a very simple explanation such as she planned for that afternoon, should compromise an established friendship?

Interrupting this self-examination the mighty but unwieldy form of Morton Crocker loomed in the white dust crescent, and his premature panama swiftly followed the curve of the low grey wall towards her gate. As his steps were heard, her mind flew to the forbidding St. Michael on his gold background in her den and she could fairly hear Harwood saying to all of us, "Three to one on the Saint, who takes me?" The jangling of the bell recalled her to Crocker, and she braced herself in the full sunlight to receive him. For a moment, as he loomed in the archway, she indulged that especial pride which we reserve for that which we might possess but austerely deny ourselves.

Her mingled moods produced an unusual softness. Crocker felt it and wondered as she gave him her hand and had him sit for a prudent moment outside. All the hot way up the valley he had had a sense of a crisis. It was odd to be summoned whither he had been drifting for four years, and now the sight of Emma disarmed, perplexed him. It seemed ominous. One finds such transparent kindness in clever people generally at parting, when one would be remembered for one's self and not for a phrase. Then Crocker for an instant glimpsed the wilder hope that the softening was for him and not for an occasion. Emma had never seemed more desirable than to-day. A white strand or two in her yellow hair, the tiny wrinkles at the corners of her steady grey eyes, and the untimely thinness of her long white fingers made him eager to ward off the advancing years at her side, to keep unchanged, as it were, these precious evidences that she had lived.

Some sense of his tenderness she must have had, for as she chatted gravely about his farming, about the lateness of the almond blossoms, about everything except people, who always tempted her sharp tongue, her manner became almost maternally solicitous. "To-day you shall have your first tea in my den, Crocker" (so much she presumed on her two years' seniority), she said at last, "and you are commanded to like my things." "What has thy servitor done to deserve this grace?" he managed to reply. "Nothing," she said, "graces never are for deserts. Or, rather, you poor fellow, you have been asked to tramp out here in this glare and really deserve to sit where it is cool." As they walked through the hall and the little drawing-room Crocker still felt uneasily that no road with Emma Verplanck could be quite as smooth as it seemed.

The den deserved its name, being a tiny brown room with a single arched window that looked askance at the cypresses and bell towers of Fiesole. Beside a couch, an Empire desk, and solid shelves of books, the den contained only a couple of chairs and the handful of things that Emma laughingly called her collection. As

Crocker took in vaguely bits of Hispano-Moresque and mellow ivories, a broad medal or so and a well-poised Renaissance bronze, a Japanese painting on the lighted wall, and one or two drawings by great contemporaries, Emma's friends, he was amazed at the quality of everything. A sense of extreme fastidiousness rebuked, in a way, his more indiscriminate zeal as a collector. Uncomfortably near him on the dark wall he began to be aware of something marvellous on old gold when tea interrupted his observations. Tea with Emma was always engrossing. The mere practice and etiquette of it brought the gentlewoman in her into a lovely salience. Her hands and eyes became magical, her talk light and constant without insistency. A symbolist might imagine eternal correspondence between the amber brew and her sunny hair. It was easy to adore Emma at tea, and generally she did not resent a discreetly pronounced homage. But this afternoon she grew almost petulant with Crocker as they talked at random, and finally laughed out impatiently: "I really can't bear your ignoring my St Michael, especially as you have never seen him before and may never see him again. St. Michael, Mr. Morton Crocker."

"My respects," smiled Crocker, as he turned lazily toward the gilded panel. There was the warrior saint, his lines stiff, expressive and hieratic, his armour glistening in grey-blue fastened with embossed gilded clasps; here and there gorgeous hints of a crimson doublet - the unmistakable enamel, the grave and delicate tension of a masterpiece by the rare Venetian, Carlo Crivelli. Crocker gasped and started from his seat, losing at once his cup, his muffin, and his manners. "By Jove, Miss Verplanck, Emma, it's my missing St. Michael. Where did you ever find it? I must have it." His toasted muffin rolled unconsidered beside the spoon at his feet. Emma retrieved the cup - one of a precious six in old Meissen - he retained the saucer painfully gripped in both hands.

"I was afraid it was," she answered, "but look well and be sure."

"Of course we must be sure. You'll let me measure it, won't you? It's the only way." Assuming his permission he climbed awkwardly upon the chair, happily a stout Italian construction, and as she watched him with a strange pity, he read off from a pocket rule: "One metre thirty-seven. A shade taller than mine, but there is no frame. Thirty-one centimetres; the same thing. Yes, it is my missing St. Michael," and as he climbed down excitedly he hurried on: "How strange to find it here. I never talked to you about it, did I? That's odd, too. I've been hunting for it for years. You didn't know, I suppose. I want it awfully. What can we do about it?" For Crocker, this fairly amounted to a speech, and before replying Emma gave him time to sit down, and thrust another cup of tea into his unwilling hands. Having thus occupied and calmed him, she said, "I'm very sorry, I hoped it would turn out to be something else. I only learned last week that you wanted it. You have seldom talked about your collecting to me. There's nothing to do about it. I wish there were. You want it so much. But I can't give it to you. That wouldn't do. And I won't sell it to you. I wouldn't to anybody, and then that wouldn't do, either. So there we are. Only think of their talk, and you'll see the situation is impossible."

Crocker's eyes flashed. "There's a lot we might do about it if you will, Emma. Damn the St. Michael. If his case is so complicated, and I don't see it, leave him out of the reckoning between us. Can't you see what I need and want?"

"They wouldn't see it, and I'm shamefully afraid of them," she said simply, and then she added indignantly, "How could you dare, to-day? I can't trust you for any perception, can I?"

Not perceiving that her scruple was belated, Crocker blurted out ruefully. "I'm an ass, and I'm sorry and I'm not. It's what I have wanted to say these many days, and perhaps it might as well be so. But I've wounded you and for that I'm more than sorry."

"Let's not talk about it," Emma said gently. "Of course I'll forgive an old friend for saying a little more than he should. Only you must stop here. You'll forgive me, too, for owning your St. Michael. I'm honestly sorry it happened so. I would dismiss him if I could, for he is likely to cost me a good friend. But he creates a kind of impossibility between us, doesn't he, and for a while it's best you shouldn't come, not till things change with you. It's kindest so, isn't it, Crocker?"

There was more debate to this effect before the impassive St. Michael, until at last Crocker agreed impatiently, "You're right, Emma, or at least you have me at a disadvantage, which comes to the same thing. And yet it's all wrong. You are putting a painted saint between yourself and a friend who wants to be more. It's logical, but it isn't human. As for their talk, they'll talk, anyhow, and we might as well stand it together. I'm probably off for a long time, Emma. I hope you'll find your St. Michael companionable. When you decide to throw him out of the window, let me know. Forgive me again. Good-by." She gave him her hand silently and followed him out into the *loggia*. As she watched him striding angrily down the valley and away, she had the air of a woman who would have cried if she were not Emma Verplanck.

* * * * *

Crocker was right, we all did talk. And naturally, for had we not all been eagerly awaiting the collision announced by the cessation of his visits and the rumour that he was bound north. In council on Dennis's terrace, however, we came to no unanimous reading of the affair. Generally, we felt that even if Emma wanted a way out, which we guessed to be the fact, she would never expose herself to our batteries, and with regret we opined that there was no way, had we wished, to divest ourselves of our collective formidableness. On all sides we divined a deadlock, with Dennis the only dissenting voice. He insisted scornfully that we none of us knew Emma, that we underestimated both her emotional capacity and her resourcefulness, and, finally, in a burst of rash clairvoyancy he declared that she would give away both the St. Michael and herself, but in her own time and manner, and with some odd personal reservation that would content us all. We should see.

Given the rare mixture of the conventional and instinctive that was Emma Verplanck, something of the sort did indeed seem probable. For ten years she had inhabited her nook, becoming as much of a fixture among us as the Campanile below. She came, like so many, for the cheapness and dignity of it primarily. Here her little patrimony meant independence, safety from perfunctory and uncongenial contacts at home, and more positively all those purtenances of the gentlewoman that she required. But, unlike the merely thrifty Italianates, she never became blunted by our incessant tea giving and receiving. With familiarity, the ineffable sweetness of the country penetrated her with ever-new impressions. She loved the overlapping blue hills that stretched away endlessly from the rim of her valley, and the scarred crag that closed it from behind. She loved the climbing white roads, her chalky brook - sung as a river by the early poets - with its bordering poplars and willows and its processional display of violets, anemones, primroses, blueflags, and roses. She loved even better that constant passing trickle of fine intelligences which feeds the Arno valley as her brook refreshed its vineyard. The best of these came gladly to her, for she was an open and a disillusioned spirit, with something of a man's downrightness under her sensitive appreciation. Hers was the calm of a temperament fined but not dulled by conformity and experience. Mrs. Dennis, whose sources of information were excellent, said it was rather an unhappy girlish affair with an unworthy cousin. Within the limits of the possible, the Verplancks always married cousins, and Emma, it was thought, had in her 'teens paid sentimental homage to the family tradition. In any case she remained surprisingly youthful under her nearly forty years. Her capacity for intellectual adventure seemed only to increase as she passed from the first glow to proved impressions of books, art, persons, and the all-inclusive Tuscan nature.

Her Stuyvesant Square aunts, who were authorities on self-sacrifice, agreed that the only sacrifice Emma had made in a thoroughly selfish life was the purchase of the St. Michael. She had found it, on a visit in Romagna, in the hands of a noble family who knew its value and needed to sell it, but dreaded the vulgarity of a transaction through the antiquaries. To Emma, accordingly, whom they assumed to be rich, they offered it at a price staggering for her, though still cheap for it. From the first she had adored it. There had been a swift exchange of despatches with New York, and the St. Michael went home with her to Florence. After that adventure the small victoria, the stocky pony, and the solemn coachman had never reappeared. Emma walked to teas or, when she must, suffered the promiscuity of the trams. To those of us who knew the store she set by her equipage its exchange for the St. Michael indicated a fairly fanatical devotion. To her aunts it meant that she had spent her principal, which, in their eyes, was an approximation to the mysterious "sin against the Holy Ghost."

It was Dennis who speculated most audaciously, and perhaps truly, about the St. Michael. When he learned that Emma secreted it in her den, where she rarely admitted anyone, he maintained that it had become her incorporeal spouse. The daintiness with which it fingered a golden sword-hilt, as if fearing contamination, symbolised the aloofness of her spirit. The solitary enjoyment of a great impression of art made her den a sanctuary, absolving her from commoner or shared pleasures. And in a manner the Saint was the type of the ultra-virginal quality she had retained through much contact with books and life. For her to sell the St. Michael, Dennis felt, would be a sort of vending of her soul, to give it away in the present instance would imply, he insisted, an instinctive self-surrender of which he judged her incapable.

To Crocker's side of the affair we gave very little thought, considering that he, after all, had created the thrilling importance of the St. Michael. But our general attitude toward the unwonted was one of indifference, and Crocker was too unlike us to permit his orbit to be calculated. The element of foible in him was almost null. None of our guesses ever stuck to him, and we had grown weary of rediscovering that anything so simple could also be so impermeable to our ingenuity. In a word, Crocker's case was as much plainer than Emma's as noonday is than twilight. When one says that he was born in Boston and from birth dedicated to the Harvard nine, eleven, or crew - as it might befall; that he was graduated a candidate for the right clubs, that he took to stocks so naturally that he quickly and safely increased an ample inherited fortune, and this without neglecting horse, or rod, or gun; finally that he carried into maturity a fine boyish ease - when this has been said all has been told about Morton Crocker except the whimsical chance that made him an Italianate.

Some reminiscence of his grand tour had beguiled a tedious convalescence and, following the gleam for want of more serious occupation, he had set sail for Naples with a motor-car in the hold. At thirty-three he brought the keenness of a girl to the galleries, the towns, and the ineffable whole thing. It was Tuscany that completed his capture. He bought a villa and, as his strength came back, began to add new vineyards and orchards to his estate. But this was his play; his serious work became collecting and more particularly, as has been hinted, the quest of the missing St. Michael. When he learned, as a man of means soon must, that good pictures may still be bought in Italy, he promptly succumbed to the covetousness of the collector, and the motor-car became predatory. Its tonneau had contained surreptitious Lottos and

Carpaccios. Its gyrations became an object of interest to the Ministry of Public Instruction. Once on crossing the Alps it had been searched to the linings. While Crocker had his ups and downs as a collector, from the first his sense of reality stood him in stead. Being a Bostonian he naturally studied, but even before he at all knew why, he disregarded the pastiches and forgeries, and made unhesitatingly for the good panel in an array of rubbish.

It was this sense for reality that impelled him to settle where the rest of us merely perched. Fifty *contadini* tilled his domain and actually began to earn out the costly improvements he had introduced. His wine and oil were sought by those who knew and were willing to pay. In the intervals of the major passion Crocker walked up and down the grassy roads superintending the larger operations. His muscular and hulking blondness - he had rowed four years - towered above the dark little men who served, feared, and worshipped him. Unlike the rest of us who preferred to live in a delightful Cloud Cuckoo Town, which happened to be Florence also, he had chosen to take root in Tuscany.

First he purged his castellated villa of the international abuses it had undergone for a century. It had hardly regained its fifteenth century spaciousness and simplicity before it began to fill up again, but this time with pictures and fittings of the time. In all directions he bought with enthusiasm, but his real vocation, after the cultivation of Emma's society, soon came to be the completion of his great and growing altar-piece by Carlo Crivelli. What is usually a frigid exercise, a mere ascertainment that the parts of a scattered ancona are at London, Berlin, St. Petersburg, Boston, etc. - a patient compilation of measurements, documents and probabilities; what is generally a mere pretext for a solid article in a heavy journal - or at best a question of pasting photographs together in the order the artist intended - Crocker converted into an eager and most practical pursuit. Bit by bit he gradually reconstituted his Crivelli in its ancient glory of enamel on gold within its ornate mouldings. The quest prospered capitally until he stuck hopelessly at the missing St. Michael. As it stood for a couple of years complete except for the void where the St. Michael should be, the altar-piece represented less Crocker's abundant resources than his tireless patience and energy. He had picked up the first fragment, a slender St. Catherine of Alexandria demurely leaning upon her spiked wheel, at a provincial antiquary's in Romagna, not far from where the ancona had been impiously dismembered. Fortunately the original Gothic frame remained to give a clue to other panels. Next, word of a Crivelli Madonna with Donors at Christie's took him posthaste to London. Frame, period and measurements proved that it was the central panel, and the tiny donors, a husband and wife with a boy and girl, indicated that the wings had contained two female and two male saints. Between the St. Lucy (which turned up more than a year later in an un-heard-of Swedish collection, and was had only by a hard exchange for a rare Lorenzo Monaco and a plausible Fra Angelico) and the sumptuous St. Augustine, which was brought to the villa in a barrow by a little dealer, there was a longer interval. Meanwhile the frame had been reconstructed, and a niche for the missing saint rose in melancholy emptiness. A little before the sensational *rencontre* in Emma's den, the chance of finding a rude pilgrim woodcut on the Quai Voltaire revealed the saint's identity. This ugly print informed the faithful that the "prodigious image" of Our Lady existed in the Church of the Carmelites at Borgo San Liberale. One might distinguish at the extreme right of the five compartments a willowy St. Michael in armour, like Chaucer's Squire in a black-letter folio, or if the identification had been doubtful, there was the name below in all letters.

When the print was shown to the scheming Harwood over the afternoon vermouth, he suspended a long discourse on the contemptible fate of being born an Anglo-Saxon, and it came over him with a blessed shock that Emma had the missing St. Michael. Penetrated by the joy of the situation, he hesitated for a moment whether to give the initiative to the man or the woman. A glance at Crocker's uncompromising sturdiness convinced him that on that side the situation might be quickly exhausted. Emma he could trust to do it full justice. Excusing himself abruptly, he made for Frau Stern's lodgings, and with the taste of Crocker's vermouth still in his faithless mouth, told her that Emma's Crivelli was no other than the missing St. Michael. To make matters sure he solemnly bound Frau Stern to secrecy. That accomplished, he strode whistling down through the purple twilight to his well-earned *fritto* at Paoli's. The next day began our wondering what Emma would do. She did, as is known, a thing that her simple Knickerbocker ancestresses would have approved - presented Crocker to the St. Michael and left the decision modestly to the men. Behind the frankness of her procedure lay, perhaps, a curiosity to see how Crocker would bear himself in a delicate emergency. It was to be in some fashion his ordeal. Thus she might at least shake the appalling equanimity with which he had passed from the stage of comrade to that of suppliant. Not that she doubted him; nobody did that, but she resented a little in retrospect his silence on the subject of the great quest. Was it possible that for these five years he had chatted only about his college pranks, his fishing trips, his orchards and vineyards, and the views? As she reviewed their countless walks and teas, it really seemed as if he had never paid her the compliment of being impersonal. Well, that was ended now at any rate. A little misgiving filled her that she had never revealed the presence of the St. Michael to so good a play-fellow. A delicacy, knowing his incorrigible zeal as a collector, had restrained her, and then, as Dennis had guessed, her den was her sanctuary, admission to which implied an intimacy difficult to concede. Whatever the merits of the case, the rupture had produced in a milieu consumed by the desire to guess what Emma would do, at least one person who was solely interested in what Crocker's next move might be. For the first time in a singularly calculable life he had become an object of genuine curiosity.

He acted with his usual simplicity. To Emma he wrote a brief note upbraiding her for fearing the voices of the valley, professing his eagerness to return when the St. Michael had been put out of the reckoning, and declaring that if it were not soon, he would willy-nilly come back and see how things were between them. It was a letter that wounded Emma, yet somehow warmed her, too, and from its reception we found her in an unwonted attitude of nonconformity to the verdicts of the valley. She began to speak up in behalf of this or that human specimen under our diminishing lenses with the unsubtle and disconcerting bluntness of Morton Crocker himself. The phenomenon kept alive our waning interest during nearly a year of waiting. As for Crocker he gave it out ostentatiously that he was bound for a wonderful Cima in Northumbria and afterward was to try dry-fly fishing on the Itchen. Beyond that he had no plans. All this was characteristically the truth; he bought the Cima, wrote of his baskets to Harwood, but stayed away past his melons, his grapes and his olives. By early winter we heard of him shooting the moose in New Brunswick, and later planning a system of art education in the Massachusetts schools, and it was not till the brisk days of March that we learned the west wind was bringing him our way again.

Meanwhile Emma had acquired a few more grey hairs and had resolutely declined to dispossess herself of the St. Michael. A couple of months after Crocker's leave-taking, a note had come to her from Crespi, the unfrocked priest and consummate antiquarian, who, to the point of improvising a *chef d'oeuvre*, will furnish anything that this gilded age demands. Crespi most respectfully begged to represent an urgent client, a Russian prince, who desired a fine Crivelli. Would the most gentle Miss Verplanck haply part with hers? The price should be what she chose to name. It was no question of money, but of obliging a client whom Crespi could ill afford to disappoint. Emma curtly declined the offer. The St. Michael was valued for personal reasons and was not for sale. Six weeks later came a more insidious suggestion. The Director of the Uffizi, learning that she possessed a masterpiece of a school sparsely represented in the first Italian gallery, pleading that such an object should not pass from Italy, and representing a number of generous art-lovers who desired to add it to the collections under his care, made the following offer, trusting, however, not to any pecuniary inducement but to her loyalty as an honorary citizen of Florence. The price named was something less than the London value, but its acceptance would have perpetually endowed the victoria, and perhaps - . If the malicious Harwood had not passed the word that the offer was a ruse of the wily Crocker, we all believed that she would have accepted. Indeed, we regretted her obduracy. It would have been such a capital way out, with no sacrifice of her scruples nor waiver of our collective impressiveness. So Harwood came in for mild reprehension, the Sage Dennis remarking with some asperity that when the gods have provided us with farces, comedies, and tragedies in from one to five acts it is unseemly to string them out to six or seven.

Early March, then, saw the deadlock unbroken. The St. Michael had not been dislodged. Emma still was unwavering so far as we knew. We were unable, had we willed, to divest ourselves of our deterrent attributes. But the situation had changed to this extent that Crocker was said to be on his way down to oversee a new system of spring tillage in person.

Emma took his approach with something between terror and an unwonted resignation. From the day when he had planted himself firmly beside her fireplace with a boyish wonder at finding himself so much at home, he had represented the incalculable in her carefully planned life. Declining to accept the attitude of other people toward her, he had almost upset her attitude toward herself. He was the first man since the scapegrace cousin who had neither feared nor yet provoked her sharp tongue. While he relished her wit, it had always been with an unspoken deprecation of its cutting edge. He gave her a queer feeling of having allowances made for her - a condescension that in anybody but this big, likable boy she would have requited with sarcasm. But against him the *cheveux de frise* she successfully presented to the world seemed of no avail. He knew it was not timber but twigs, and that at worst one was scratched and not impaled. Day by day she watched the cropping of the long line of flaming willow plumes that escorted her brook toward the level. The line dwindled as the shorn pollards gave up their withes to bind the vines to the dwarf maples. She felt the miles between herself and Crocker lessening, and (at rare moments) her scruples ready to be garnered for some sweet and ill-defined but surely serviceable use. But she would not have been Emma Verplanck if the manner of her not impossible surrender had not troubled her more than the act itself. Any lack of tact on the part of the husbandman might still spoil things. She had a whimsical sense that any one of the flaming willows might refuse its contribution to the vineyard should the pruner approach with anything short of a persuasive "*con permesso*."

Crocker's "by your leave" was so far from persuasive that it left her with a panicky desire to run away - again a new sensation. He wrote:

"DEAR EMMA -

"We have had an endless year to think it over, and the only change on my side is that I need you more than ever. I will go away for real reasons, for your reasons, but for no others. If it is only their talk that separates us, their talk has had twelve good months and shall have no more. I must see you. May I come tomorrow at the old hour?

"As always yours,

"MORTON CROCKER."

Something between wrath and dismay was the result of this challenge. She sat down to answer him according to his impudence, and the words would not come. The greatness of the required sacrifice came over her and therewith the desire to temporise. The voice of many Knickerbocker ancestresses spoke in her, and between herself and a real emergency she interposed the impenetrable buckler of a conventionality. She wrote:

"PENSIOIN SCHALCK, Bad Weisstein, Austrian Tyrol.

"MY DEAR CROCKER -

"It would be pleasant to see you and talk over your trip, but you see by this address it is for the present impossible. As always,

"Cordially yours,

"EMMA VERPLANCK."

When Crocker found Emma's valley as effectually barred as if a battery guarded the approaches, he gave way to a deep resentment. Instinctively hating anything like a trick, to be tricked by Emma at this point was intolerable. His gloom was such that he confided to the malicious Harwood a profound disgust with the irreality of the life Italianate. The *podere* should be sold as soon as it could be put in order. Such pictures as the Italian Government coveted, it should keep, the rest should go to the Museum at Boston. He himself would grow orange trees in North Cuba where there were things to shoot and, thank heaven, no civilisation.

Harwood came breathlessly to Dennis's with the tale, gloating openly that there was to be a seventh act if not an eighth.

A long hard day with his bailiff and the peasants restored Crocker's poise. He looked for the hundredth time over into Emma's valley and divined her attitude. Dreading an interview, she had left the way open to parley. She virtually pleaded for a delay. It was a new and, in a way, delightful sensation to be feared. For the first time in any human relation he exploited a personal advantage and wrote, addressing Bad Weisstein:

"DEAREST EMMA -

"You have wanted a delay. Well, you have it - probably a week already. Make the most of it, for two weeks from this date - I give you time to recover from your journey - I am coming for tea in the old way. Meanwhile you can hardly imagine the impatience of

"Yours more than ever,

"MORTON CROCKER."

Whether Crocker or Emma was more miserable during the fortnight even Dennis could not have told. But there was in his woe something of the sublime stolidity of the man who is going to stand up to be shot or reprieved, whereas she suffered the uncertainty of the soldier who has been drawn to make up the "firing party" for a comrade. She feared that she would not have courage enough to despatch him, and then she feared she would. Meantime the days passed, and she woke up one morning with an odd little shiver reminding her that it was no longer possible to get a note to him by way of Bad Weisstein. Nor had she the heart to move to a nearer coign of constructive absence. Of half measures she was, after all, a foe. Her determination to send Crocker away daily increased, and the implacable St. Michael seemed to command that course. "You are not for him. You represent a whole artificial world in which he cannot breathe. I, the finest incarnation of the most exquisite mannerism of a bygone time, am your spiritual spouse, and you may not lightly renounce me. You have devoted yourself to graceful irrealities and must now abide by your choice." Thus the St. Michael had spoken in a dream in the troubled hours before daybreak, and when Emma went to her den late the next morning she confronted him and admitted, "You are right, St. Michael. It's all true." That afternoon Crocker was coming for tea, and if her New York aunts could have known, even they would have granted that, for the second time in a thoroughly selfish life, Emma was displaying capacities for self-sacrifice.

As Emma and Crocker shook hands that afternoon, one might see that both had aged a little, but he most. Something of the appealing boyishness had gone out of his eyes. He had become her contemporary. A certain moral advantage, too, had passed to his side and she, whose prerogative it had been to take the leading part, now waited for him to begin. As if on honour to do nothing abruptly, he sketched his year for her - his sports and committees, his kinsfolk and hers; their fresh, invigorating, half-made land. She listened almost in silence until he turned to her and said:

"With me, Emma, it is and always will be the same. You know that. Has anything changed with you?"

"I don't think so, Crocker. How can I tell? I'm glad you're here, in spite of the shabby trick I've played you. Let me say just that I'm heartily glad to see an old friend."

"No, I must have more than that or less. I want much more than that."

"You want too much. You want more than I can give to anybody. O! Why can't you see it all? You are alive, even here in Florence but, I, I am no longer a real person that can love or be loved. Can't you see that I am only a sensibility that absorbs the sweetness of this valley, a mere bundle of scruples and fears, a weather-cock veering with the talk of the rest of them? Think of that and take back what you have thought about me."

"Emma, you admit a need, and that is very sweet to me. You want some one to strengthen you against all this that you call the valley. Mightn't that helper be I?"

"You shan't be committed to anything so hopeless."

"It isn't as hopeless as it seems. The strength of the valley is only in its weakness, and we shall be strong together."

"I have forgotten how to be strong, for years I have only been clever."

"You'd be dull enough with me as you well know. I can do that for both. But don't talk as if there were some fate between us. There can be none except your indifference, and I believe you do care a little and will more."

"Of course, I care, Crocker, but not as you wish. You have refreshed me in this opiate air. You have represented the real country I have exchanged for this illusion, the real life I might have lived had I been braver or more fortunate. But you can have no part in what I have come to be. Go, for both our sakes."

"Not for any such reason. I can't surrender my happiness for a phrase; I can't leave you to these delusions about yourself."

"It is no delusion; I wish it were. It's in my blood and breeding. For generations my people have lived the unreal life. I am the fine flower of my race, and in coming to this valley of dreams and this no-life I am merely fulfilling a destiny - a fate, as you say - and coming to my own."

"But Emma, the worthy Verplancks?"

"No, listen to me. For generations the Verplancks have been what people expected them to be, incarnate formulas of etiquette and timid living. They took their colour from the gossiping society in which they seemed to live. They prudently married other Verplancks, cousins or cousins' cousins. They hoarded their little fortunes without increasing them, and if what they called the rabble had not peopled New York and raised the price of land, which my people were merely too stolid to sell, we should long ago have gone under in penury. We have led nobody and made nothing, but have been maintained by stronger forces and persons, toward whom we have always taken the air of doing a favour. That mistake at least I shall not make with you, Crocker. I want you to feel the full nullity of me. As I see you now I have a twinge because my great grandfather, who was a small banker, would have called yours, who was a farmer - you see I have looked you up - not 'Mister' but 'My Good Man.'"

For a moment she paused, and Crocker groped for a reply. "All this may be true, Emma," he said at last, "and yet mean very little to you and me. Besides, I'm quite willing you should call me your Good Man. In fact, I'd rather like it."

"You must take me seriously - you shall. I cannot marry. I'm married already. Dennis says I am. Come and see my bridegroom." And she fairly dragged the bewildered Crocker into her den and set him once more before the missing St. Michael.

"There he is, an incarnated weakness and fastidiousness. His hand is too delicate to draw his own sword. If he really cast out Satan, it must have been by merely staring him down. His helmet rests with no weight upon his curled and perfumed locks - his buckles are soft gold where iron should be. He represents the dull, collective, aristocratic intolerance of Heaven for the only individualist it ever managed to produce. He pretends to be a warrior and is as feminine as your St. Catherine. He is the imperturbable champion of celestial good form, and Dennis, who sees through things, says he is my spiritual husband. He is the weakest of the weak and is too strong for you, Crocker."

For a space that seemed minutes they faced each other, Emma excited, with a diffused indignation that defied impartially the missing St. Michael and the puzzled man before her; Crocker with a perplexity that renewed the old boyish expression in his eyes. He seemed to be thinking, and, as he thought, the tension of Emma's attitude relaxed, she forgot to look at the St. Michael and wondered at the even, steady patience of the big likable boy she was dismissing. She pitied him in advance for the futile argument he must be revolving. She had despatched him as in duty bound and was both sorry and glad.

But his counterplea when it came was of a disconcerting briefness and potency. He said very slowly, "Yes, I see it all. There is your spiritual husband; there are they" (indicating the valley with a sweep of a big hand), "and there are you, Emma, caught in a web of baffling and false ideas; and here am I, a real man who loves you, fearing neither the St. Michael nor them" (another gesture) "nor your doubts. I set myself, Morton Crocker, your lover, against them all and take my own so."

There was a frightened second in which his sturdy arms closed about her. There was a little shudder, as the same big hand that had defied the valley sought her head and pressed it to his shoulder. When Emma at last looked up the mockery she always carried in her eyes had given place to a new serenity, and her hand reached up timidly for his.

Crocker and Emma - we now instinctively gave him the precedence - were inconsiderate enough to remove themselves without making clear the fate of the no longer missing St. Michael. We still speculated indolently as to the nature of the afterpiece in which we assumed this ex-hero of our comedy might yet appear. Then we learned that Emma was to be married without delay from the stone manor house under the Taconics where her people had dwelt since patroon days. Only a handful of friends with Crocker's nearest kin and her inevitable New York aunts were to be present. These venerable ladies had admitted that in marrying, even opulently, out of the family, Emma had once more shown velleities of self-sacrifice. Then we heard of Crocker and Emma on his boat along the coast "Down East." Later we were shocked by rumours of a canoe trip through Canadian waterways. Hereupon the usually benevolent Dennis protested as he glanced approvingly at the well-kept Tuscan landscape. "Crocker needn't rub it in," he opined. "Why, it's the same scrubby spruce tree from the Plains of Abraham to James's Bay-and Emma, who hated being bored! Why, it's marriage by capture; it's barbaric." "It's worse; it's rheumatic," shuddered Harwood as he declined Marsala and took whisky. "But he'll have to bring her back to civilisation some time, if only to hospital. We shall have her again." "He will bring her back, but we shall never have her again," said Dennis solemnly. "She has renounced us and all our works." "Renouncing our works isn't so difficult," smiled Mrs. Dennis, and then the talk drifted elsewhere, to new Emmas who were just beginning to eat the Tuscan lotus.

Before the year had turned to June again we had nearly forgotten our runaways, when a quite unusual activity about her villa and Crocker's warned us that they were coming back. Harwood had seen in transit a box which he thought corresponded to the St. Michael's stature, but was not sure. In a few days came a circular note from Crocker through Dennis saying that they were fairly settled and he glad to see any or all of us. She, however, was still fatigued by the journey and must for a time keep her room.

Harwood straightway volunteered to undertake the preliminary reconnaissance, while Frau Stern engaged to penetrate to Emma herself.

On a beatific afternoon we sat in council on Dennis's terrace awaiting the envoys. Below, the misty plain rose on and on till it gathered into an amber surge in Monte Morello and rippled away again through the Fiesolan hills. Nearer, torrid bell-towers pierced the shimmering reek, like stakes in a sweltering lagoon. In the centre of all, the great dome swam lightly, a gigantic celestial buoy in a vaporous sea. The spell that bound us all was doubly potent that day. The sense of a continuous life that had made the dome and the belfries an inevitable emanation from the clean crumbling earth, lulled us all, and we hardly stirred when Harwood bustled in, saying, "Cheer up. I have seen Crocker, and it isn't there." "You mean," said the cautious Dennis, "that Crocker still possesses only the hole, aperture, frame, or niche that the missing St. Michael may yet adorn." "I only know that it isn't there now," growled Harwood. "I deal merely in facts, but you may get theories, if you must have them, from Frau Stern, who heroically forced her way to Emma over Crocker's prostrate form."

As he spoke we heard Frau Stern's timid, well-meaning ring, and in a moment her smile filled the archway.

"We don't need to ask if you have news," cried Mrs. Dennis from afar.

"If I haf news. Guess what it is. It is too lovely. You cannot think? Well, there will be a baby next autumn, what you call it?" "Michaelmas, I suppose," grunted Harwood through his pipe-smoke and subsided into indifference.

"All this is most charming and interesting, Frau Stern," expostulated Dennis, "but, as our enthusiastic friend Harwood delicately hints, what we really let you go for was to locate the Missing St. Michael." "I haf almost forgot that," she apologised as she nibbled her *brioche*, "Emma was so happy. But for the bothersome St. Michael there is no change. I saw it in what she calls her new den. She laughed to me and said, 'I cannot let him have it, you see, you would all say he married me for it.'"

"Bravo!" shouted Dennis and Harwood in unison, and the Sage added with unction, "So she has not been able to renounce us utterly."

"It is not now for long," rejoined Frau Stern, "it is only to the time we haf said." "Michaelmas," repeated Harwood disgustedly.

"Yes, that is it," she pursued tranquilly, "Emma told me in confidence, 'To Crocker I cannot give it because of you all, but to our child I may, and it shall do with it what it will.' Now do you prevail, Misters Dennis and Harwood?"

"We are a bit downcast but not discomfited," acknowledged Dennis, while Harwood remained glumly within his smoke. "Emma has escaped us, but she still pays us the tribute of a subterfuge. It is enough, we will forgive her, even if her way lies from us dozers here. For to-day the same sunshine drenches her and us. It is a bond. Let us enjoy it while we may."

THE LUSTRED POTS

"Haul away, Sam. This is the real thing" came from the depths of the well. Sam Cleghorn stumbled in the gloom towards the windlass, avoiding on the way a rude handpump and two heaps of dirt and broken pottery that sloped threateningly upon the low curb, where balanced a perforated disc of marble, the great bottom-stone of the well. All these properties caught a little light from a beam that came through a slit in the wall, casting most of its uncertain bloom up into a low groined vault, the heavy round arches of which were separated from squat piers by clumsy brackets. Outside at the level of the reticulated stone floor one could hear the rushing of a river. As Cleghorn leaned over the well-mouth before seizing the crank, a glimmer of yellow light flooded his face and again came up the hollow impatient cry, "Haul away, Sam. This lot's a good one, and it's mine." Replying "All right, Dick," Cleghorn bent to the crank. With much creaking the coils crept along the spindle and the light burden began to rise jerkily.

* * * * *

Although neither the well nor the vaulted cellar chamber belonged to Sam Cleghorn or to Dick Webb, their presence and actions there were not surreptitious. Stanton Mayhew, who ignorantly owned the well, had given them plenary permission to pump and dig, mildly pitying their apparent lunacy. The palace above was his in virtue of his sensible preference for living twice as well on the Arno for half the cost on the Hudson. This rule of two, like so many foreign residents of Florence, he unquestioningly obeyed, and it constituted practically the whole of his philosophy and maxims. Hence he was not the man to prize a Tuscan well dug in the fourteenth century, cleaned perhaps never, and gradually filled to the brim with what the forwardlooking past benightedly took for rubbish. So when Cleghorn and Webb made him an overture for the right to clean the well, he had genially replied, "Why, go ahead, boys, and enjoy yourselves. It's you who ought to be paid, but for your healths' sake you really ought to wait till I've punched some decent windows through that damp cellar wall and let the air in."

If neither Sam nor Dick waited even a day, it was because each was a bit afraid that the other would begin alone. College mates, collectors both, they were fast friends in a way and rivals beyond dispute. Their common taste for antiquity and adequacy of means had made their graduate course chiefly one of travel. And when travel wore out its novelty they naturally settled in the easiest, as the least exacting, European city, occupying two halves of one floor in the same palace. Their apartments started full, and quickly overflowed with objects of curiosity and art - all old, for their knowledge was considerable; some fine, for neither was without taste. But taste neither had in any austere sense, for they collected art much as a dredge collects marine specimens. Nothing came amiss to them. Wood, ivory, silver, bronze, marble, plaster - they repudiated no material or period. Stuffs, glass, pictures, porcelains, potteries - it was all one to them so the object were old and rare. Inevitably, then, they had come to primitive pots, and simultaneously, for they not only watched each other closely, but almost read each other's minds. And when they came to primitive pots it was certain that they would beg, borrow, or steal a well, since in old wells, and cisterns, besides less mentionable places, primitive pots abide. Many pots were there, as we shall see, from the first, and the maids and children of the centuries, by way of concealing breakages, have usually made notable secondary contributions. So when amiable Stanton Mayhew freely conceded a most ancient well to Cleghorn and Webb, it was like receiving Pandora's box, with the difference that the well might safely be opened.

Here had ensued a most delicate negotiation concerning the division of the spoil. A mathematical partition of the fragmentary material that an old Italian well contains is extremely difficult if at all possible. After much debate it was agreed that after they struck pay dirt, each should dig in turn, each to have the bucketful that came under his trowel or fingers. Scattered fragments of the same pot and other complications were to be adjudicated by Mayhew, whose ignorance and disinterestedness were safe to assume. But the well gave up quantities of non-contentious matter before Mayhew's services were required. The first five feet had revealed nothing but fragments of kitchen pottery of our time and a fairly perfect hoopskirt of Garibaldian date. A little lower had emerged the skeleton of a cat. Similar tragedies were in evidence, on an average, at every quarter century of depth. Between the second and third cat, lay Ginori imitations of Sevres and Wedgewood, scraps too of gilded glass - the earnest of better things below. Five cats down, some eighteenth-century apothecary pots, damaged but amenable to repair, had inaugurated the alternation of buckets under the agreement. It were tedious to follow the ascending scale of excellence as the digging went deeper. Enough to say that below the mixed ingredients and the nethermost cat they found a homogeneous layer of beautiful fourteenth-century shards, affording many buckets full, and promising delicate adjudication to the referee.

Before the lustred pots themselves shed a baleful gleam over this narrative, something should obviously be said about Italian wells and why they contain pots. Beyond those casually acquired from careless or secretive servants, there is, if the well be old and of good make, a certain number of intact pieces put in to serve as a filter. Often a group of pitchers or similar crocks is imprisoned between the two bottom-stones. Sometimes there are two such layers. After this filter had been made there was frequently scattered a bushel or more of small shards above. From these by careful sorting complete or nearly complete pieces may be recovered. Through all this mass of whole or broken pottery the water had to find its way up, for the cement sides of an Italian well are watertight. Thus, barring the indiscretions of housemaids and cats, the early Italians drank pure water.

Naturally Cleghorn and Webb were conversant with these refinements of mediaeval hydraulics. In fact when Webb, the sturdier of the two, hauled up the bottom-stone all dripping, Cleghorn promptly declared that in the sense of the contract it was a bucketful; hence his first go at the now uncovered pots. So heated grew the debate, that finally the grimy excavators climbed to the upper air and appealed to Mayhew, who promptly denied the quibble, deciding that stones and pots were not interchangeable. The diversion drew attention from the great perforated disc itself, and as the sullen Cleghorn let the exultant Webb down upon the ancient pots, it lay badly bestowed near the curb on the crumbling slope of a rubbish heap. And now Cleghorn with bitterness of heart was reeling up Webb's find. As the coils broadened on the windlass a small iron bucket rose above the parapet, brimming with something that glinted metallically under the dirt. Beside the bucket flapped the rude swing in which the entrances and exits of the partners were made. As Cleghorn grasped the bail and swung the precious cargo clear of the well, came up once more the voice of Webb: "Hustle, Old Man, I'm keen to see them, they feel good."

Good they were indeed. Cleghorn, who for fifteen years had haunted shops and museums had never seen the like in equal compass. As he took them cautiously one by one and held them high in the uncertain light, each revealed a desirable point. Here was a coat of arms, a date, the initial of an owner. There were grotesque birds and beasts. Differing in form and colour, the entire lot agreed in possessing that dull early Italian lustre, which perhaps accidental and less distinguished than that of Spain, is even dearer in a collector's eyes. They hinted of all enameled things that come out of the East - of the peacock reflections of the tiles of Damascus and Cordova, of the franker polychromy of Rhodian kilns, of the subtler bloom of the dishes of Moorish Spain, of the brassier glazes of Minorca and Sicily - all these things lay enticingly in epitome in these lustred Italian pots, as they glimmered with a furtive splendour. Yes, they were a good lot, thought Cleghorn as he placed them reverently on the flagging. It was the find of a lifetime. A man with nothing else in his cupboard must be mentioned respectfully among collectors from Dan to Beersheba.

Again the impatient voice of Webb below: "Hurry up, I say. It's getting cold: the water is gaining."

"All right," called Cleghorn, giving a few strokes of the pump, but never taking his eyes from the lustred pots. Then as if by a sudden inspiration he asked, "Any more in that lot, Dick?"

"Not a one," cried Webb jubilantly, "there was just a bucketful and a squeeze at that. But there may be others beneath. There's another bottom-stone, and it's your next turn. But why don't you hurry up?"

A scowl passed over Cleghorn's thin face set unswervingly towards the pots. They glimmered in the shadow with an unholy phosphorescence - green, blue, carmine, strange purplish browns. So the glittering coils of the serpent may have bewildered our first Mother. There were other pots below, reflected Cleghorn, yes, but there never could be again such a batch as these. And then his dazed eye for a second left the fascinating pots, and mechanically searched the vaulted chamber. To his excited gaze the rubbish heaps centring about the curb seemed already in movement. The massive bottom-stone overhung the parapet, resting only on loose dirt and shards. With horror he noted that a breath might send it down. If it slipped, whose were the lustred pots? Against his will the phrase said itself over and over again throbbingly behind his eyes, and again he forgot everything in the vision of the lustred pots.

"Damn it, hurry up," came thunderously from below. Cleghorn stumbled with a curious hesitation between the crank and the poised bottom-stone. The clumsy movement loosened a handful of shards which went clattering down; the great stone slid, caught on the parapet, and hung once more in uncertain oscillation. Profanity unrestrained transpired from the mouth of the well.

It was a tremulous Cleghorn that sent down the bucket and reeled up an irate and vociferous Webb. Words abounded without explanations, and blows seemed possible, when Cleghorn, as it were apologetically raised a pitcher and a bowl into the shaft of light that came through the oubliette. "They're all like that, Dick," he protested. "It's your lucky day. I congratulate you." It was a silenced and mollified Webb that clutched at the pots, and noted wisely that every one had been brushed by the peacock's tail. With a kind of pity at last he turned to the deprecating Cleghorn and said, "That was an awkward business of yours about the shards, and the bottom-stone there is a pretty sight for a man who left it so and went down to work under it, but one couldn't wait for such pots as these. On my soul, Old Man, if you had dumped it all down on me I could hardly have blamed you."

Welcomed with a loud laugh by its maker, the joke jarred on Cleghorn, who merely answered, "It's very good of you, Dick, to say so."

"But there may be quite as good ones below," pursued Webb genially. "We'll rest up a bit and then you have your go and finish the job."

"If you don't mind, Dick, I'd rather not," was the

embarrassed answer. "The fact is I'm too nervous and absentminded for this work." He looked down into the blackness with a shudder and said. "No, I don't want to go down there again. One can't tell what might happen there."

"Then you've dropped your nerve. Sorry for it," came from a baffled and disgusted partner, but as he spoke a smile drew across the broad, amiable face, and he added insinuatingly, "Then the rest are mine, Old Man?"

"Yes they're yours fast enough."

"It's mighty good of you, Sam. I won't forget it. I'll share sometime on a good thing like this. I'm all ready to go down again when you've had a smoke. Only we'll set that stone right and you'll be more careful about the shards."

"If you'll excuse me, Dick, I'd rather not." Cleghorn looked at his watch. "You see I ought to be out of these duds already. I have a very particular tea outside. Didn't I tell you about it? I'll send Mayhew down to help."

"All right, just as you please," was the indifferent reply. But as Cleghorn turned up the narrow steps, Webb muttered perplexedly, "To funk at this point and for a tea! The man is touched or in love."

* * * * *

Webb with Mayhew's dispassionate aid made a considerable haul below the second stone, though in truth there was nothing there to compare with the first lot. The batch of lustred pots is the pride of his eye, and when it is suggested that he values them highly he answers, "Well rather, they're pretty good, you know, and then they nearly cost me a broken head. I was so keen for them that I set a big stone where it might easily have tumbled on me." Then the rest of the anecdote, which Cleghorn, in whose presence it frequently is told, never hears with complete equanimity. The causes of his uneasiness I do not engage to analyse, for, unlike Webb, Cleghorn is imaginative and difficult.

THE BALAKLAVA CORONAL

As the dinner wore on endlessly, I consoled myself by the thought of the Balaklava Coronal. There in the toastmaster's seat was Morrison who had bought it, at my right loomed Vogelstein who had sold it, far across, towards the foot of the board, sat the critic Brush in whose presence I understood the infamous sale had been made. I missed only Sarafoff, the marvellous peasant-silversmith, who wrought the coronal in his prison workshop in the Viennese ghetto. Now there was nothing strange about Vogelstein's selling it, nor yet about Morrison's buying it; only the making of it by the illiterate Sarafoff and the silence of Brush when it was sold required explanation. Vogelstein, who breathed heavily beside me, undoubtedly held the secret. I felt so hopeful that time and the champagne which we were drinking for the sake of art would give him to me that I took no pains meanwhile to disturb his elaborate indifference to my presence.

Between him and me little love was lost. As the editor of a moneylosing art magazine in the interior, it was my duty occasionally to visit his galleries. After such visits the remnant of my New England conscience usually forced me to diminish or actually to spoil many a sale of the dubious or merely fashionable antiquities in which he dealt. But in the main my power to harm him was slight. He held in a knowing grip the strings of his patrons' vanity and taste. So he regarded me with something between scorn and uneasiness - as a pachyderm might take a predatory bee. For the sake of my steady production of the honey of free advertising he forgave a sting from which he was after all immune. At the beginning of the dinner he had greeted me with what was meant for a civility and then had relapsed into silence. To escape the loquacity of my other neighbour I gave myself to parallel observation of Vogelstein and Morrison - the great dealer and his greater customer.

Both plainly belonged to the same species and it pleased my whim to symbolise them as a mastodon and a rogue elephant. Morrison, the dreaded agent and operator, was unquestionably the finer creature. He moved more precisely and with a sense of wieldy power. His phrases cut where Vogelstein's merely smote. His bigness had something genial about it. He looked the amateur, and indeed does not the rogue elephant trample down villages chiefly for the joy of the affray? One felt that something more than Morrison's preposterous winnings had been involved in the clashes of railroads and cataclysms on the exchange which had for years past been his major recreation. Vogelstein, though evidently of coarser fibre, belonged to the same formidable breed. The mastodon, we must suppose, lacked much of the finesse of the rogue elephant of later evolution. And Vogelstein's Semitism was of the archaic, potent, monumental type. His abundant fat looked hard. For all the sagging double chin, his jaw retained the character of a clamp. Among the strong race of art dealers he was feared. Whole collections not single objects were his quarry. He paid lavishly, foolishly, counting as confidently on the ignorance and vanity of his clients, as ever Morrison upon the brute expansion of the national wealth. But Vogelstein looked and was as completely the professional as Morrison the amateur. There remained this essential difference that if nothing could be too big to stagger Vogelstein, nothing likewise could be too small to deter him. I knew his shop, or rather his palace, and had observed the relish with which he could shame a timorous art student into giving three prices for a print. It afforded him no more pleasure, one could surmise, to impose a false Rembrandt at six figures upon a wavering iron-master, or, indeed to unload an historic but rather worthless collection upon Morrison himself. For Vogelstein was after all of primitive stamp, to wit the militant publican. So he took toll and plenty, it mattered little where or whence.

To Morrison and Vogelstein no better foil could be imagined than Brush. If they recalled the tusked monsters that charged in the van of Asiatic armies, his analogue was the desert horse. Small, spare, sensitive, shy, his every posture suggested race, training, spirit, and docility. His *flair* for classical art had become proverbial. By mere touch he detected those remarkable counterfeits of Syracusan coins. It was he who segregated the Renaissance intaglios at Bloomsbury only the winter before he exposed the composite figurines at Berlin. To him the Balaklava Coronal must have proclaimed its nullity as far as its red gold could be seen. For that matter the coronal was a bye-word, and why not? The same dealers who had landed the more famous Tiara in the Louvre had the selling of it. The greater museums in Europe and America had refused it at a bargain. On Fifth Avenue and the Rue Lafitte all the dealers were joking about the Balaklava

Coronal. The name of Sarafoff, its maker, had even become accepted slang. For a season we "Sarafoffed" our intimates instead of hoaxing them. And in the face of all this Vogelstein had sold the Coronal to Morrison under Brush's very nose. It seemed so wholly incredible that I began counting Vogelstein's heavy respirations, to make sure I was really awake.

Then the pale, tense mask of Brush - so isolated in the apoplectic row across the table - calmed me. That he was Vogelstein's or anyone's tool was unthinkable. Mercenary suspicions, to be sure, had been put about, but those who knew him merely laughed at such a notion. Vogelstein also laughed, shaking volcanically within, whenever the Coronal, the genuineness of which he still maintained, was mentioned. And he always treated Brush with a curious and almost tender condescension, much in fact as the mastodon might have regarded that fragile ancestor of the horse, the five-toed protohippos.

I have neglected to explain that the occasion which brought me at one table with such major celebrities as Morrison, Vogelstein, and Brush was a public dinner in behalf of civic art. For just as we find the celestial compromised by the naughty Aphrodite, so we distinguish two antithetical sorts of art. There is a bad private art which is produced for dealers and millionaires and takes care of itself, and there is a virtuous public art which we hope to have some day and meanwhile has to be taken care of by special societies. It was one of these that was now dining for the good of the cause. Under the benevolent eye of Morrison, our acting president, we had put pompano upon a soup underlaid with oysters, and then a larded fillet upon some casual tidbit of terrapins. Whereupon a frozen punch. Thus courage was gained, the consecrated sequence of sherry, hock, claret and champagne being absolved, for the proper discussion of woodcock in the red with a famous old burgundy - Morrison's personal compliment to the apostolate of civic art.

At the dessert, Morrison himself spoke a few words. The little speech came brusquely from him, and no one who knew his rapacity for the beautiful could doubt his faith in the universal superlatives he now advocated. Our art, he held, must weigh with our mills and railroads, else our life is out of balance. We never grudged millions to burrow beneath New York for light, or for drink or speed, why then should we grudge them for the beautiful inutilities that might make the surface of the city splendid. A craving for fine objects was his own dearest emotion, he wanted to see cities, states, and the nation ready to spend with equal fervour. It all came apparently to a matter of spending. Morrison entertained no doubt that an imperious demand would create an abundant supply of what he called the best art. Whether we were to transport bodily the great monuments of Europe to America, or merely were to supply beauty off our indigenous bat, was not clear from Morrison's address, and possibly was not wholly so in his own mind. But the talk was solid and forceful, and I could hear Vogelstein grunt with inward joy when he contemplated the city, the state, and the nation in their predicted role as customers. I too felt that a real if an incoherent voice had spoken, and that if civic art were indeed to come, it would be through such neo-Roman visionaries as Morrison.

Then the mood changed and a willowy, hirsute, and

earnest reviver of tapestry weaving rose and pleaded for the "City Beautiful," castigating the Philistine the while, and looking forward to a time when "the pomp, and chronicle of our time should be splendidly committed to illumined window and pictured wall," with some slight allusion to "those ancient webs through which the Middle Ages still speak glowingly to us."

About midway in the speech Morrison, who had another public dinner down the avenue slipped away. As he nodded "See you later perhaps" I marked the adoring eye and smile of Vogelstein, and then the great folds settled back into their places about his mouth and my neighbour once more gave an uneasy attention to the weaver of beautiful phrases, meanwhile drinking repeated glasses of burgundy. Soon his huge form heaved with an inarticulate discontent, and as the speaker sat down amid perfunctory applause Vogelstein snorted twice into the air.

"It is rather absurd, as you say," I ventured.

"It's sickening," wheezed Vogelstein. "Why can't he sell his tapestries without all that talk?"

"Oh, he enjoys the talk and probably believes it, and you and I do better after all to hear his talk than to see his tapestries." A mastodonic chuckle welcomed this mild sally. The burgundy was taking effect.

As the diners rose stiffly or alertly, according to their several grades of repletion, Vogelstein attached himself to me almost affectionately. "Do stop in the cafe and talk to me," he urged. "It's queer, here are a lot of my customers, some of my artists, besides you literary chaps, and except Morrison, nobody wants to talk to me. Morrison and I, we understand each other. It's early yet. Come along with me and talk. I've wanted to talk to you for a long time, but always was too busy in my place. You see you writers don't buy, in fact those that know almost never do. It's really queer."

Knowing the might of burgundy when a due foundation of champagne has been laid, I hardly took this effusion as personal to myself, but I also saw no reason, too, why I should not profit by the occasion. "I'll gladly chat with you, Mr. Vogelstein," I answered, "but you must let me choose the subject. We will talk about the Balaklava Coronal."

As he led me into the elevator by the arm he whispered "All right, Old Man, but why? You know just as much as I about it."

There was no chance to reply until he had selected his table and ordered two Scotches and soda. "Yes, I know something about it," I said at last; "everyone does apparently except Morrison. I know that Sarafoff made the Coronal, but I don't know who taught him how to make it, nor yet how Morrison was idiot enough to buy it, when anybody could have told him what it was, nor yet how Brush came to let it be sold. These are the interesting parts of the story, and I'll drink no drink of yours unless you tell."

At the mention of idiocy in connection with Morrison Vogelstein shuddered and raised a massive deprecating hand. The gesture was arrested by the entrance of Brush, who with a slight nod to us passed to a distant corner. Suddenly Vogelstein's expression had become one beaming, condescending paternalism. "Good man but impracticable," he muttered. "Thinks knowing it is everything. Knowing it is something, but selling it is the real thing. Now I hardly know at all, not a tenth as much as Brush, not a half as much as you even, but so long as I can sell, I don't really care to know. What's the use?"

"But you did know about the Balaklava Coronal and you sold it too," I interrupted. "How did you dare?"

"That's my secret - but here are our drinks. A bargain's a bargain. How funny it is to be talking truth. Why, much of it would make even your job difficult."

"And yours impossible, but we're not getting to the Coronal," I insisted.

"As for that," responded Vogelstein obligingly, "the first thing was of course the making. You know all about Sarafoff yourself. Well, he only did the work. It was Schoenfeld who put in the brains. You don't know him? Few do. Great man though. University professor of archaeology, trouble with a woman, next trouble with money, now one of us. Yes Schoenfeld thought it out and saw it through."

"And certainly made a good job of it," I admitted.

"As you see, we wanted something unique - something that could not be compared with anything in the museums."

"Precisely," I interposed, "Product of the local, semi-barbaric school of the Crimea."

"You've hit it," grinned Vogelstein. "Scythian

influence, to take the professors. Schoenfeld said we must have that. And that's why it had to be found at Balaklava."

"But it had to look Scythian too. How did you manage that?"

"Oh, that was Sarafoff's business. He had been a servant and then a novice at one of the monasteries of Mount Athos. Could make beautiful tenth-century Byzantine madonnas. I've sold some. Then he carved ikons in wood, ivory, silver, or what came. His things really looked Scythian enough to those who didn't know their modern Greece and Russia. So we set him to work in a back alley of Vienna at three kroners a day - double pay for him - and Schoenfeld ran down from Petersburg now and then to coach him."

"You could trust him?" I inquired, recalling how Sarafoff had subsequently won fame by confessing to his most famous forgery.

"As much as one can anybody. You see he doesn't speak any civilized language, and at that time we couldn't tell that the Tiara would spoil him as it did the entire deal."

"But Schoenfeld's coaching?" I suggested. Vogelstein here winked solemnly and drank deeply from his tall glass. "First I want to tell you all about Sarafoff," he persisted, "of course we had him watched all the same, and whenever he got an evening off, which was seldom, we had him filled up with schnapps. He was a quiet drunk which is an excellent thing, Sir." As I nodded assent to this great truth, he continued: "Yes Schoenfeld, as I was saying, managed everything.

Wonderful scholar. You would respect him I'm sure. Why, every bit of the pattern of the Coronal was taken from some real antique, every word of the inscription too." "Wasn't that a bit dangerous?" "With Schoenfeld in charge, not so very. Everything was taken from little Russian museums that even you critics don't visit. Almost no published thing was used, you see."

"Then there was Sarafoff" -

"To give it all that quaint Scythian look," Vogelstein added joyously. "Yes, we had just the best brains and the best hands for the job, and it was beautiful." "Better than the Tiara?"

"Yes, far better. The Tiara was all a mistake, as I told Schoenfeld; it was too big and too good to be true. Except for Steinbach, who fell in love with its queerness and chipped in some money, we never could have sold it to a museum. And it was a bad thing to have it there, it aroused opposition, it was bound to be exposed. I was always against it, and sure enough it spoiled the game for us. But the Balaklava Coronal that was just right. It had a sort of well-bred modest beauty. We should have begun instead of ending with it. Yes, Sir, there never was a more beautiful thing, a more plausible thing, a finer object to sell than the Balaklava Coronal."

As he bellowed the word and beat the table in confirmation, Brush looked over from his corner apprehensively. "Quietly, Mr. Vogelstein," I hinted, "this is between ourselves, and we might be overheard."

"That's right," he admitted, and moodily lit another

cigar. "Where were we?" he asked uneasily. "Oh yes, we were at the Tiara. Now the Coronal and what we could have sold on the strength of it was worth ten of the Tiara, and if it hadn't been for the cursed thing, we could have landed the Coronal as a starter in any one of half a dozen museums."

"As a matter of fact they were all shy of it."

"Of course. Once the Tiara was being looked into, the museum game was up, and there was only Morrison left." Vogelstein lurched around nervously. "He may drop in soon," he explained. "I'd like to make you acquainted."

Ignoring the offer, I persisted, "You've got to the interesting point at last. Tell me why there was only Morrison left. To begin with Morrison knows something about such matters, and next he can have the best advice for the asking. And yet you tell me that Morrison was the only great collector in the world to whom that notoriously false bauble could be sold."

Vogelstein swayed uncomfortably in his chair, puffed, swallowed, cleared his throat, and said, "There are some things one can't say right out; you know that as well as I, but I can say this: there are many great and enterprising collectors in America, and Morrison is the only one who never doubts anything he has once bought."

"An ideal client then."

"Quite so. You see the others get worried by the critics. That means exchanging, refunding - all sorts of trouble."

"But Morrison never?"

"Never; he's a true sport. He never squeals."

"Doesn't have to because he doesn't know he's hurt."

"That's right," concluded Vogelstein, his face corrugating into one ample, contented smile.

"Then the big game reduces itself into selling to Morrison."

"That's more or less it, Sir. For a critic you have a business head."

"You will excuse a rather personal question, but how do you feel about selling your best customer at enormous prices objects which you know to be false?"

"It's a fair question since we are talking between ourselves, and you shall have a straight answer. First my business isn't just a nice one. In the nature of the case it wouldn't do for sensitive people. I suppose you and Brush, for instance, couldn't and wouldn't make much out of it. Then as regards Morrison, I'm not so sure he could complain if he knew. I give him the things he likes and the treatment he likes at the prices he likes. What more can any merchant do?"

I saw the subject rapidly exhausting itself and tried one more tack. "Yes, it's simpler than I supposed," I admitted, "but it doesn't seem quite an every-day thing to sell the Balaklava Coronal to anybody under Brush's nose."

"It's easier than you think," echoed Vogelstein. "You

don't know Morrison. Hope he'll look in to-night. You ought to meet him."

My last bolt was shot. It was my turn to sit silent and drink. What could be this strange infatuation of the hardheaded Morrison, this avowedly simple magic of the grossly cunning Vogelstein? As I pondered the case I noticed Brush give a startled glance towards the entrance, heard heavy steps behind us, and then a deep voice saying, "Hallo again, Vogelstein, I'm lucky not to be too late to catch you."

Vogelstein lumbered to his feet and muttered an introduction. We all took our seats, as the headwaiter bustled obsequiously up to take Morrison's order of champagne. As if also obeying Morrison's nod, but reluctantly, Brush crawled over from his corner, a scarcely deferential attendant transporting his lemonade.

While casual greetings and some random talk went on I tried to picture the scene we must present. Neither Brush nor myself is contemptible physically or in other ways, yet we both seemed curiously the inferiors of these troglodytic giants. Our scruples, the voluntary complication of our lives, seemed to constitute at least a disadvantage when measured against the primitiveness, perhaps the rather brutal simplicity, of our companions.

It was Morrison who cut these reflections short. "You will excuse me, gentlemen," he said, "for introducing a matter of business here, but the case is pressing and it may even interest you as critics of art." We nodded permission and he continued, "It's about the Bleichrode Raphael, as of course you know, Vogelstein. I like it, I want it, but I hear all sorts of things about it, and frankly it strikes me as dear at the price. How do you feel about it?"

At the mention of the Bleichrode Raphael, Brush and I started. The forgery was more than notorious. The Bleichrode panel had begun life poorly but honestly as a Franciabigio - a portrait of an unknown Florentine lad with a beretta, the type of which Raphael's portrait of himself is the most famous example. The picture hung long in a private gallery at Rome and was duly listed in the handbooks. One day it disappeared and when it once more came to light it had become the Bleichrode Raphael. Its Raphaelisation had been effected, as many of us knew, by the consummate restorer Vilgard of Ghent, and for him the task had been an easy one. It had needed only slight eliminations and discreet additions to produce a portrait of Raphael by himself far more obviously captivating than any of the genuine series. Soon the picture vanished from Schloss Bleichrode, and it became anybody's guess what amateur had been elected to become its possessor. The museums naturally were forewarned.

While this came into Brush's memory and mine, Vogelstein's countenance had become severe, almost sinister, and he was answering Morrison as follows:

"Mr. Morrison, I have offered you the Bleichrode Raphael for half a million dollars. You will hear all sorts of gossip about it. Doubtless these gentlemen (indicating us) believe it is false and will tell you so (we nodded feebly). But I offer it not to their judgment but to yours. You and I know it is a beautiful thing and worth the money. I make no claims, offer no guarantee for the picture. You have seen it, and that's enough. If you don't want it, it makes no difference to me, I can sell it to Theiss (the great Parisian amateur, Morrison's only real rival), or I will gladly keep it myself, for I shall never have anything as fine again."

Morrison sat impassively while Vogelstein watched him narrowly. Brush and I felt for something that ought to be said yet would not come. At the end of his speech, or challenge, Vogelstein's expression had softened into one of the most courtly ingenuousness, now it hardened again into a strange arrogance. His eyes snapped as he continued with affected indifference, "Since you have raised the question, Mr. Morrison, the Bleichrode Raphael is yours to take or leave - to-night."

There was a pause as the two giants faced each other. Then Morrison smiled beamingly, as one who loved a good fighter, and said, "Send it round tomorrow, of course I want it. Well, that's settled, and if these gentlemen will spare you, I'll give you a lift down town."

Vogelstein's arrogance melted once more into fulsomeness as he said, almost forgetting his Goodnight to us, "I'm sure it's very good of you, Mr. Morrison."

The forms of Morrison and Vogelstein almost blocked the generous intercolumnar space as shoulder to shoulder they moved away between the yellow marble pillars and under the green and gold ceiling. The brown leather doors swung silently behind them, and we were left together with our amazement.

"Never mind, Old Fellow," said Brush at last. "It's the

first time for you. You'll get used to it. It's my second time; I happened to be there, you know, when the Balaklava Coronal was sold."

SOME REFLECTIONS ON ART COLLECTING

Morally considered, the art collector is tainted with the fourth deadly sin; pathologically, he is often afflicted by a degree of mania. His distinguished kinsman, the connoisseur, scorns him as a kind of mercenary, or at least a manner of renegade. I shall never forget the expression with which a great connoisseur - who possesses one of the finest private collections in the Val d'Arno - in speaking of a famous colleague, declared, "Oh, X -! Why, X - is merely a collector." The implication is, of course, that the one who loves art truly and knows it thoroughly will find full satisfaction in an enjoyment devoid alike of envy or the desire of possession He is to adore all beautiful objects with a Platonic fervour to which the idea of acquisition and domestication is repugnant. Before going into this lofty argument, I should perhaps explain the collection of my scornful friend. He would have said: "I see that as I put X - in his proper place, you look at my pictures and smile. You have rightly divined that they are of some rarity, of a sort, in fact, for which X - and his kind would sell their immortal souls. But I beg you to note that these pictures and bits of sculpture have been bought not at all for their rarity, nor even for their beauty as such, but simply because of their appropriateness as decorations for this particular villa. They represent not my energy as a collector, nor even my zeal as a connoisseur, but simply my normal activity as a man of taste. In this villa it happens that Italian old masters seem the proper material for decoration. In another house or in another land you might find me employing, again solely for decorative purposes, the prints of Japan, the landscapes of the modern impressionists, the rugs of the East, or the blankets of the Arizona desert. Free me, then, from the reproach implied in that covert leer at my Early Sienese." Yes, we must, I think, exclude from the ranks of the true zealots all who in any plausible fashion utilise the objects of art they buy. Excess, the craving to possess what he apparently does not need, is the mark of your true collector. Now these visionaries - at least the true ones - honour each other according to the degree of "eye" that each possesses. By "eye" the collector means a faculty of discerning a fine object quickly and instinctively. And, in fact, the trained eye becomes a magically fine instrument. It detects the fractions of a millimetre by which a copy belies its original. In colours it distinguishes nuances that a moderately trained vision will declare non-existent. Nor is the trained collector bound by the evidence of the eye alone. Of certain things he knows the taste or adhesiveness. His ear grasps the true ring of certain potteries, porcelains, or qualities of beaten metal. I know an expert on Japanese pottery who, when a sixth sense tells him that two pots apparently identical come really from different kilns, puts them behind his back and refers the matter from his retina to his finger-tips. Thus alternately challenged and trusted, the eye should become extraordinarily expert. A Florentine collector once saw in a junk-shop a marble head of beautiful workmanship. Ninety-nine amateurs out of a hundred would have said. "What a beautiful copy!" for the same head is exhibited in a famous museum and is reproduced in pasteboard, clay, metal, and stone *ad nauseam*. But this collector gave the apparent copy a second look and a third. He reflected that the example in the museum was itself no original, but a school-piece, and as he gazed the conviction grew that here was the original. Since it was closing time, and the marble heavy, a bargain was struck for the morrow. After an anxious night, this fortunate amateur returned in a cab to bring home what criticism now admits is a superb Desiderio da Settignano. The incident illustrates capitally the combination of keenness and patience that goes to make the collector's eye.

We may divide collectors into those who play the game and those who do not. The wealthy gentleman who gives *carte blanche* to his dealers and agents is merely a spoilsport. He makes what should be a matter of adroitness simply an issue of brute force. He robs of all delicacy what from the first glow of discovery to actual possession should be a fine transaction. Not only does he lose the real pleasures of the chase, but he raises up a special clan of sycophants to part him and his money. A mere handful of such - amassers, let us say - have demoralised the art market. According to the length of their purses, collectors may also be divided into those who seek and those who are sought. Wisdom lies in making the most of either condition. The seekers unquestionably get more pleasure; the sought achieve the more imposing results. The seekers depend chiefly on their own judgment, buying preferably of those who know less than themselves; the sought depend upon the judgment of those who know more than themselves, and, naturally, must pay for such vicarious expertise. And, rightly, they pay dear. Let no one who buys of a great dealer imagine that he pays simply the cost of an object plus a generous percentage of profit. No, much-sought amateur, you pay the rent of that palace in Bond Street or Fifth Avenue; you pay the salary of the gentlemanly assistant or partner whose time is at your disposal during your too rare visits; you pay the commissions of an army of agents throughout the world; you pay, alas! too often the cost of securing false "sale records" in classic auction rooms; and, finally, it is only too probable that you pay also a heavy secret commission to the disinterested friend who happened to remark there was an uncommonly fine object in Y -'s gallery. By a cheerful acquiescence in the suggestions that are daily made to you, you may accumulate old masters as impersonally, as genteelly, let me say, as you do railway bonds. But, of course, under these circumstances you must not expect bargains.

Now, in objects that are out of the fashion - a category including always many of the best things - and if approached in slack times, the great dealers will occasionally afford bargains, but in general the economically minded collector, who is not necessarily the poor one, must intercept his prey before it reaches the capitals. That it makes all the difference from whom and where you buy, let a recent example attest. A few years ago a fine Giorgionesque portrait was offered to an American amateur by a famous London dealer. At $60,000 the refusal was granted for a few days only, subject to cable response. The photograph was tempting, but the besought amateur, knowing that the authenticity of the average Giorgione is somewhat less certain than, say, the period of the Book of Job, let the opportunity pass. A few months after learning of this incident, I had the pleasure of meeting in Florence an English amateur who expatiated upon the beauty of a Giorgione that he had just acquired at the very reasonable price of $15,000. For particulars he referred me to one of the great dealers of Florence. The portrait, as I already suspected, was the one I had heard of in America. Forty-five thousand dollars represented the difference between buying it of a Florentine rather than a London dealer. Of course, the picture itself had never left Florence at all, the limited refusal and the rest were merely part of the usual comedy played between the great dealer and his client. On the other hand, if the lucky English collector had had the additional good fortune to make his find in an Italian auction room or at a small dealer's, he would probably have paid little more than $5,000, while the same purchase made of a wholly ignorant dealer or direct from the reduced family who sold this ancestor might have been made for a few hundred francs. With the seekers obviously lie all the mystery and romance of the pursuit. The rest surely need not be envied to the sought. One thinks of Consul J.J. Jarves gradually getting together that little collection of Italian primitives, at New Haven, which, scorned in his lifetime and actually foreclosed for a trifling debt, is now an object of pilgrimage for European amateurs and experts. One recalls the mouse-like activities of the Brothers Dutuit, unearthing here a gorgeous enamel, retrieving there a Rembrandt drawing, fetching out a Gothic ivory from a junk-shop. One sighs for those days, and declares that they are forever past. Does not the sage M. Eudel warn us that there are no more finds - *"Surtout ne comptez plus sur les trouvailles."* Yet not so long ago I mildly chid a seeker, him of the Desiderio, for not having one of his rare pictures photographed for the use of students. He smiled and admitted that I was perfectly right, but added pleadingly, "You know a negative costs about twenty francs, and for that one may often get an original." Why, even I who write - but I have promised that this essay shall not exceed reasonable bounds.

For the poor collector, however, the money consideration remains a source of manifold embarrassment, morally and otherwise. How many an enthusiast has justified an extravagant purchase by a flattering prevision of profits accruing to his widow and orphans? Let the recording angel reply. And such hopes are at times justified. There have been instances of men refused by the life insurance companies who have deliberately adopted the alternative of collecting for investment, and have done so successfully. Obviously, such persons fall into the class which the French call charitably the *marchand-amateur*. Note, however, that the merchant comes first. Now, to be a poor yet reasonably successful collector without becoming a *marchand-amateur* requires moral tact and resolution. The seeker of the short purse naturally becomes a sort of expert in prices. As he prowls he sees many fine things which he neither covets nor could afford to keep, but which are offered at prices temptingly below their value in the great shops. The temptation is strong to buy and resell. Naturally, one profitable transaction of this sort leads to another, and soon the amateur is in the attitude of "making the collection pay for itself." The inducement is so insidious that I presume there are rather few persistent collectors not wealthy who are not in a measure dealers. Now, to deal or not to deal might seem purely a matter of social and business expediency. But the issue really lies deeper. The difficulty is that of not letting your left hand know what your right hand does. A morally ambidextrous person may do what he pleases. He keeps the dealer and collector apart, and subject to his will one or the other emerges. The feat is too difficult for average humanity. In nearly every case a prolonged struggle will end in favour of the commercial self. I have followed the course of many collector-dealers, and I know very few instances in which the collection has not averaged down to the level of a shop - a fine shop, perhaps, but still a shop. I blame no man for following the wide road, but I feel more kinship with him who walks scrupulously in the narrow path of strict amateurism. Let me hasten to add that there are times when everybody must sell. Collections must periodically be weeded out; one may be hard up and sell his pictures as another in similar case his horses; artists will naturally draw into their studios beautiful objects which, occasion offering, they properly sell. With these obvious exceptions the line is absolutely sharp. Did you buy a thing to keep? Then you are an amateur, though later your convenience or necessity dictates a sale. Did you buy it to sell? Then you are a dealer.

The safety of the little collector lies in specialisation, and there, too, lies his surest satisfaction. To have a well-defined specialty immediately simplifies the quest. There are many places where one need never go. Moreover, where nature has provided fair intelligence, one must die very young in order not to die an expert. As I write I think of D -, one of the last surviving philosophers. Born with the instincts of a man of letters, he declined to give himself to the gentler pursuit until he had made a little competence at the law. As he followed his disinterested course of writing and travel, his enthusiasm centred upon the antiquities of Greece and Rome. In the engraved gems of that time he found a beautiful epitome of his favourite studies. For ten years study and collecting have gone patiently hand in hand. He possesses some fifty classical gems, many of the best Greek period, all rare and interesting from material, subject, or workmanship, and he may have spent as many dollars in the process, but I rather doubt it. He knows his subject as well as he loves it. Naturally he is writing a book on intaglios, and it will be a good one. Meanwhile, if the fancy takes him to visit the site of the Bactrian Empire, he has only to put his collection in his pocket and enjoy it *en route*. I cannot too highly commend his example, and yet his course is too austere for many of us. Has untrammelled curiosity no charms? Would I, for example, forego my casual kakemonos, my ignorantly acquired majolica, some trifling accumulation of Greek coins, that handful of Eastern rugs? Could I prune away certain excrescent minor Whistlers? those bits of ivory cutting from old Italy and Japan? Those tarnished Tuscan panels? - in truth, I could and would not. Yet had I stuck to my first love, prints, I should by this time be mentioned respectfully among the initiated, my name would be found in the card-catalogues of the great dealers, my decease would be looked forward to with resignation by my junior colleagues. As it is, after twenty years of collecting, and an expenditure shameful in one of my fiscal estate, I have nothing that even courtesy itself could call a collection. In apology, I may plead only the sting of unchartered curiosity, the adventurous thrill of buying on half or no knowledge, the joy of an instinctive sympathy that, irrespective of boundaries, knows its own when it sees it. And you austerely single-minded amateurs, you experts that surely shall be, I revere if I may not follow you.

We have left dangling from the first paragraph the morally important question, Is collecting merely an habitual contravention of the tenth commandment? Now, I am far from denying that collecting has its pathology, even its criminology, if you will. The mere lust of acquisition may take the ugly form of coveting what one neither loves nor understands. This pit is digged for the rich collector. Poor collectors, on the other hand, have at times forgotten where enterprise ends and kleptomania begins. But these excesses are, after all, rare, and for that matter they are merely those that attach to all exaggerations of legitimate passion. As for the notion that one should love beautiful things without desiring them, it seems to me to lie perilously near a sort of pseudo-Platonism, which, wherever it recurs, is the enemy of life itself. As I write, my eye falls upon a Japanese sword-guard. I have seen it a thousand times, but I never fail to feel the same thrill. Out of the disc of blued steel the artisan has worked the soaring form of a bird with upraised wings. It is indicated in skeleton fashion by bars extraordinarily energetic, yet suavely modulated. There must have been feeling and intelligence in every touch of the chisel and file that wrought it. Could that same object seen occasionally in a museum showcase afford me any comparable pleasure? Is not the education of the eye, like the education of the sentiments, dependent upon stable associations that can be many times repeated? Shall I seem merely covetous because I crave besides the casual and adventurous contact with beauty in the world, a gratification which is sure and ever waiting for me? But let me cite rather a certain collector and man of great affairs, who perforce spends his days in adjusting business interests that extend from the arctic snows to the tropics. His evenings belong generally to his friends, for he possesses in a rare degree the art of companionship. The small hours are his own, and frequently he spends them in painting beautiful copies of his Japanese potteries. It is his homage to the artisans who contrived those strange forms and imagined those gorgeous glazes. In the end he will have a catalogue illustrated from his own designs. Meanwhile, he knows his potteries as the shepherd knows his flock. What casuist will find the heart to deny him so innocent a pleasure? And he merely represents in a very high degree the sort of priestliness that the true collector feels towards his temporary possessions.

And this sense of the high, nay, supreme value of beautiful things, has its evident uses. That the beauty of art has not largely perished from the earth is due chiefly to the collector. He interposes his sensitiveness between the insensibility of the average man and the always exiled thing of beauty. If we have in a fractional measure the art treasures of the past, it has been because the collector has given them asylum. Museums, all manner of overt public activities, derive ultimately from his initiative. It is he who asserts the continuity of art and illustrates its dignity. The stewardship of art is manifold, but no one has a clearer right to that honourable title. "Private vices, public virtues," I hear a cynical reader murmur. So be it. I am ready to stand with the latitudinarian Mandeville. The view makes for charity. I only plead that he who covets his neighbour's tea-jar - I assume a desirable one, say, in old brown Kioto - shall be judged less harshly than he who covets his neighbour's ox.

Horace Walpole
Horatio Alger, Jr.
Howard Pyle
Howard R. Garis
Hugh Lofting
Hugh Walpole
Humphry Ward
Ian Maclaren
Israel Abrahams
J.G.Austin
J. Henri Fabre
J. M. Barrie
J. Macdonald Oxley
J. S. Knowles
J. Storer Clouston
Jack London
Jacob Abbott
James Allen
James Lane Allen
James Andrews
James Baldwin
James DeMille
James Joyce
James Oliver Curwood
James Oppenheim
James Otis
Jane Austen
Jens Peter Jacobsen
Jerome K. Jerome
John Burroughs
John F. Kennedy
John Gay
John Glasworthy
John Habberton
John Joy Bell
John Milton
John Philip Sousa
Jonathan Swift
Joseph Carey
Joseph Conrad
Joseph Jacobs
Julian Hawthrone
Julies Vernes
Justin Huntly McCarthy
Kakuzo Okakura
Kenneth Grahame
Kate Langley Bosher
L. A. Abbot
L. T. Meade
L. Frank Baum
Laura Lee Hope
Laurence Housman
Leo Tolstoy
Leonid Andreyev
Lewis Carroll
Lilian Bell
Lloyd Osbourne
Louis Tracy
Louisa May Alcott
Lucy Fitch Perkins
Lucy Maud Montgomery
Lydia Miller Middleton
Lyndon Orr
M. H. Adams
Margaret E. Sangster
Margaret Vandercook
Maria Edgeworth
Maria Thompson Daviess
Mariano Azuela
Marion Polk Angellotti
Mark Overton
Mark Twain
Mary Austin
Mary Cole
Mary Rowlandson
Mary Wollstonecraft
Shelley
Max Beerbohm
Myra Kelly
Nathaniel Hawthrone
O. F. Walton
Oscar Wilde
Owen Johnson
P.G.Wodehouse
Paul and Mable Thorn
Paul G. Tomlinson
Paul Severing
Peter B. Kyne
Plato
R. Derby Holmes
R. L. Stevenson
Rabindranath Tagore
Rahul Alvares
Ralph Waldo Emmerson
Rene Descartes
Rex E. Beach
Richard Harding Davis
Richard Jefferies
Robert Barr
Robert Frost
Robert Gordon Anderson
Robert L. Drake
Robert Lansing
Robert Michael Ballantyne
Robert W. Chambers
Rosa Nouchette Carey
Ross Kay
Rudyard Kipling
Samuel B. Allison
Samuel Hopkins Adams
Sarah Bernhardt
Selma Lagerlof
Sherwood Anderson
Sigmund Freud
Standish O'Grady
Stanley Weyman
Stella Benson
Stephen Crane
Stewart Edward White
Stijn Streuvels
Swami Abhedananda
Swami Parmananda
T. S. Ackland
The Princess Der Ling
Thomas A. Janvier
Thomas A Kempis
Thomas Anderton
Thomas Bailey Aldrich
Thomas Bulfinch
Thomas De Quincey
Thomas H. Huxley
Thomas Hardy
Thomas More
Thornton W. Burgess
U. S. Grant
Valentine Williams
Victor Appleton
Virginia Woolf
Walter Scott
Washington Irving
Wilbur Lawton
Wilkie Collins
Willa Cather
Willard F. Baker
William Makepeace
Thackeray
William W. Walter
Winston Churchill
Yei Theodora Ozaki
Young E. Allison
Zane Grey

www.ingramcontent.com/pod-product-compliance
Lightning Source LLC
LaVergne TN

LVHW090613110826
845146LV00001B/369

* 9 7 8 1 4 2 1 8 0 4 3 9 2 *